No Telephone to Heaven

MICHELLE CLIFF

Vintage International

Vintage Books
A Division of Random House, Inc. · New York

First Vintage International Edition, March 1989

Copyright © 1987 by Michelle Cliff

All rights reserved under International and Pan-American Copyright Conventions. Published in the United States by Random House, Inc., New York. Originally published, in hardcover, by E.P. Dutton, a division of NAL Penguin Inc., in 1987.

Library of Congress Cataloging-in-Publication Data
Cliff, Michelle.
No telephone to heaven.
Reprint. Originally published: New York: Dutton, 1987.
I. Title.
PR9265.9.C55N6   1988   813   87-40500
ISBN 0-679-73942-4 (pbk.)

Page 212 constitutes an extension of this copyright page.

Manufactured in the United States of America
10 9 8 7 6 5 4 3 2

For Adrienne

ACKNOWLEDGMENT

This book could not have been completed without the support of the National Endowment for the Arts and the Artists Foundation of Massachusetts—to them I am extremely grateful.

A glossary of Jamaican terms begins on page 209.

Something inside is laid wide like a wound,

some open passage that has cleft the brain,
some deep, amnesiac blow. We left
somewhere a life we never found,

customs and gods that are not born again,
some crib, some grill of light
clanged shut on us in bondage, and withheld

us from that world below us and beyond,
and in its swaddling cerements we're still bound.

—DEREK WALCOTT, "Laventille"

1

___

RUINATE

Ruinate: "This distinctive Jamaican term is used to describe lands which were once cleared for agricultural purposes and have now lapsed back into . . . 'bush.' An impressive variety of herbaceous shrubs and woody types of vegetation appears in succession, becoming thicker and taller over the years until 'high ruinate' forest may emerge. . . . . Ruinate of all forms is an all-too-frequent sign on the Jamaican landscape, despite population pressure on the land" (B. Floyd, *Jamaica: An Island Microcosm*, pp. 20–21).

It was a hot afternoon after a day of solid heavy rain. Rain which had drenched them and seemed not to have finished with them, but only to have taken itself off somewhere to return soon, replenished, with a new strength. The promise of another deluge was suspended in the afternoon half-light. The sun—hanging somewhere behind the sky, somewhere they could not find it—was unable to dry the roadbed or the thick foliage along the mountainside, so the surface stayed slick-wet, making driving a trial.

An open-backed truck was making its ascent through the Cockpit Country with a great deal of effort, slipping and sliding upward. As the cab of the truck tried to hug the mountain, the driver turned the wheel full circle—a massive effort—against the direction the road seemed to want to pull them, and the truck's back rattled and swung from side to side, alternately slapping and rattling against the rock face, hardness only thinly veiled with moss, then swaying and rattling its burden outward, into the center of the narrow, loosely graveled road, suddenly, with all the weight of its burden threatening to tear the cab from its mooring, long ago rusted and old, and to send the back of the truck flying wildly into the deep-green crevasse.

The trees which arced the road and the vines which wrapped them dripped into the back of the truck, and the rainwater gathered into pools where a black tarpaulin fell into folds and gullies.

At each curve the driver took care to sound his horn. That frequent blast and the constant rattle of the truck bounced through the valley rimmed by the mountains, losing themselves in the soft green and mixing with the harsh metallic voices of cling-cling blackbirds, questioning, it seemed, who these people were and asking what was their purpose here—all sounding against the steady *drip-drip* of the water.

There were at least twenty people in the back, standing, hanging on to the slatted sides, paint worn and wood splintery by now, managing to flatten themselves enough to leave room for the tarpaulin—and the goods it protected—in the center. With each turn they held their muscles tight, trying to create a force to counter the centrifuge of the truck back.

These people—men and women—were dressed in similar clothes, which became them as uniforms, signifying some agreement, some purpose—that they were in something together—in these clothes, at least, they seemed to blend together. This alikeness was something they needed, which could be important, even vital, to them—for the shades of their skin, places traveled to and from, events experienced, things understood, food taken into their bodies, acts of violence committed, books read, music heard, languages recognized, ones they loved, living family, varied widely, came between them. That was all to be expected, of course—that on this island, as part of this small nation, many of them would have been separated at birth. Automatically. Slipped into places where to escape would mean taking your life into your own hands. Not more, not less. Where to get out would mean crashing through barriers positioned by people not so unlike yourself. People you knew should call you brother, sister.

A light-skinned woman, daughter of landowners, native-born, slaves, emigrés, Carib, Ashanti, English, has taken her place on this truck, alongside people who easily could have hated her.

The people around her had a deep bitterness to contend with. Dressed as they were, they might move closer. Sleeping on the ground, squatting at the roadside, evoking the name of Nanny, in whose memory they were engaged in this, they might move closer. Their efforts were tender. They were making something new, approached not without difficulty, with the gravest opposition; the bitterness, the fury some held, could be strip-mined, no need to send the shaft deep at all.

Like when it was time for a backra to stand guard while some of the others, the darker ones, slept—or tried to sleep. Sometimes someone slept with one eye open.

Of course, it was never only a matter of appearance, symbol. Not at all. They were also dressed—a practical matter, a matter of survival—but it was all—the whole damned blasted t'ing—a matter of survival. They were dressed to blend with the country around them—this dripping brown and green terrain.

This dripping group of pale and dark people standing in the back of a rickety, noisy old truck was little more than a band. But their survival dress could make them feel, seem to be, an army. So they hoped. "It is no mystery/ We making history," someone hummed in dub. Yes.

What was it they wore? Why make so much of it? It's simple.

Khaki pants and shirts for one thing, some with sweat stains embracing their armpits and blossoming across their backs, as the heat smoked up from the valley.

Khaki was not new to them. Some of the men had worn khaki once before, when, under the crown and among the vestiges following independence, they were enrolled in the state schools spread across the island or the public schools in Kingston.

How many stiff bolts of the stuff had been spun to outfit the empire? The soldiers and the schoolboys. Loyalty signaled by their crispness. Their epaulets, the only interruption of brightness in clothes the color of dust, signifying where they belonged. Whether to St. George's or Calabar, Anchovy or Shooter's Hill.

Now the purpose of khaki had turned for them. Alikeness had been a goal back in those days too, but for quite different reasons. And when the state-educated boys grew up and worked as gardeners or casual laborers or distillery workers or cane-cutters, they wore khaki still, the only difference being that the pants' legs were long and the epaulets had been removed. The public-school boys, from George's or Calabar, had other choices.

The people on the truck wore khaki—and they wore discarded American army fatigues, stolen from white kids high on dope, plugged into machines sending our music into their heads, sleepyheads, on the beach at Negril or Orange Bay. Why these sleepy-headed kids, left behind after Sunsplash or Jamfest had finished, chose to wear old army clothes was another matter, to do with another country—and the people on the truck did not care at all about these children and had no difficulty stealing from them. They were nuisances, only rarely useful, bodies to be stepped across—should a wallet be visible in the pocket, so much the better. There might be one of Papa's credit cards tucked in, or at the very least a plastic case of American Express traveler's checks. Were they caught by one of the sleepyheads in the act of lifting a jacket, the sleepyheads seemed genuinely hurt, pathetic. "But, man, we love you. And the grass, man, it's good." "Bullshit, your honor. We don't need you here." Poor little Americans, after the ad had promised JAMAICA, A WORLD OF CULTURE WITHOUT BOUNDARIES, to be told they were not welcome. Were hated deeply, by some. Poor little Americans—had they harmed anyone?

Some in the group had managed to obtain camouflage

jackets, surplus from that other place, another soldier's name still taped to the breast pocket, and they wore these heavy things even in the heat. Perhaps as talismans, with the hope that those who wore them might have a protection the others did not have—beyond the protective coloration which hid a lizard on a croton leaf in broad sun. They wore the jackets in a strict rotation, with only the medical officer, formerly a nurse at Kingston Hospital, owning one to herself. Her name was Harriet; in the jacket she became Thorpe. There were five other jackets—and they called each by the name on the pocket: Johnson, Washington, Skrobski, Diaz, Morrissey. The names from a B-picture—RKO-Radio or Columbia or Republic—like the ones they used to see in triple features at the open-air Rialto before it was torn down. GIs fortified with Camels talking about baseball while stalking the silent, treacherous Jap.

The camouflage jackets, names and all, added a further awareness, a touch of realism, cinematic verité, that anyone who eyed them would believe they were faced with *real* soldiers. True soldiers—though no government had ordered them into battle—far from it. But this is how the camouflage made them feel. As the gold and green and black knitted caps some wore—a danger because the bright gold would sing out in the bush—made them feel like real freedom-fighters, like their comrades in the ANC—a cliché, almost screenplayed to death, *Viva Zapata!* and all that—but that *is* what they were, what they *felt* they were, what they *were* in fact. Their reason emblazoned in the colors of their skulls. *Burn!*

The black tarpaulin at the center of the back of the truck concealed stacks of guns, automatic rifles, and a few machine guns, boxes and belts of ammunition, grenades—and bags of rice, boxes of sugar, bottles of aerated water, tins of condensed milk, baskets of tomatoes, yams, and bananas.

They had traded for the guns and ammunition the ganja they cultivated on an abandoned farm in the parish of St.

Elizabeth. The farm once belonging to the grandmother of one of the members of the band—the daughter of landowners, taking her place now in the truck back.

The grandmother was long since dead, and the farm had been left by the family to the forest. To *ruination,* the grandmother would have said. The family, but one, were scattered through America and England and had begun new lives, some transplanted for more than twenty years, and no one wanted to return and reclaim the property—at least not until now.

By the time the group had decided to take the farm as a place to stay and conceal themselves, the forest had already moved in—long-time—around the house, edging the verandah. Mahogany. Broadleaf. Mosquito wood. Shadbark. Silk-cotton. Guango. Cashew. Lignum vitae. Ebony. Wild pine. The forest had obliterated the family graves, so that the grandmother and her husband, and their son who died before them, were wrapped by wild vines which tangled the mango trees shading their plots, linking them further to the wild trees, anchoring their duppies to the ground.

The garden the grandmother had planted was gone. Her carefully planned flowers, a devotion of fifty years, a way, she said, of giving something back to the Almighty, as she had given her son to Him, as He had given His son to her— these flowers, chosen for color and texture and how each would set off the next, revealing splendor and glory, her order, her choices, reflecting the order, the choices, of His universe, had been haphazardly supplanted by wilder and brighter ones, exploding disorder into her scheme. A wild design of color was spun through her garden and across her grave, masking the stonecutter's spare testament to her devotion: S E R V A N T   O F   G O D. A flame-of-the-forest sparked the disorder, as the heavy jasmine scented the ruination.

The forest had been moving up from the river for twenty years. In that time the hillside of coffee and shade trees had also been taken over, and thick-trunked vines and wild trees

8

settled into the hillside and strangled the precious, delicate coffee bushes. The citrus which had been cultivated on the flat acre by the river had been completely overshadowed by Ethiopian apples and wild bamboo—towering green stalks, shutting out any sun.

Where the grandmother had grafted the citrus—bitter Seville giving way to sweet Valencia—the graft remained staunch. But higher up the tree, in pursuit of light, the fruit returned to what it was, and sweetness was caught between the bitter and the long-lived.

There was no forgiveness in this disorder. Sasabonsam, fire-eyed forest monster, dangled his legs from the height of a silk-cotton tree.

Beneath the bush was a network of shelters where small animals hid themselves. They didn't take kindly to these intruders. Like the birds in the dripping valley, the animals wondered who these people were and what was their purpose in this place. The animals knew this only as a wild, unhumaned place. In the tops of coconut trees, far above the ribbon of river which split the land, rats had burrowed into the coconuts, living inside the nut and licking the jelly off the walls for sustenance. When one home dried out, the rat had only to leap to another pattern of fronds, for the trees had grown quickly during the rampage of the forest, and find a fresh and green unopened coconut.

For company, the rats had one another, and the black and yellow swallowtail, who sat on the flat fronds at the tops of the trees warming itself in preparation for flight.

Now, the place had a different pattern of sounds altogether. The only sound that remained from the grandmother's time was the rush of the riverwater, but that, which had once sounded clearly through the open grove of citrus, was muffled by the new thick growth and fainter, more distant than before. It competed with the creak and rustle of the coconut fronds, the noises of the animals moving through the undergrowth, the population of wild birds, and the steady gnawing of the rats making nests.

9

It took the soldiers months to clear enough bush to have land enough to plant. At first they used machetes, fixing themselves in a line against the green, the incredibly alive green, swinging their blades in unison, sometimes singing songs they remembered from the grandmothers and grandfathers who had swung their own blades once in the canefields. Some passing the blades to their children, and grandchildren. The music made another human sound, combining with the human sound of metal against green, serving notice on the animals that the invaders were here to stay.

Back and forth across the wildness of the forest that faced them, the soldiers moved, in the evenings honing their blades to prepare for the morning's task.

Swinging their blades against the tough bush, some of them thought about their grandparents, thought: yes, this is for them too. And for their mothers: our mothers who fathered us when the men were called away or drifted off. Although we may never be able to tell those who are still alive. They may never know who we really were. Some of them think we are living off the streets of Kingston. Some of them think we are teaching school in Mandeville. Some of them think we have made a better life in America. They might hate us if they knew. Might think the shadow-catcher get us. Or Old Hige slip from her skin and suck our souls.

When they had weakened the bush enough, and made enough clearance by chopping down the trees in their way, slicing the vines which embraced the trees, they brought in pigs to root up the stumps, taking some by night from the farm of a backra man a few miles off. The man was at his main residence in Kingston; this was his country house, and the old caretaker, toothless and black-up, a figure in stained khaki pushed against a stucco wall, did not even stir when the pigs squealed. They took it upon themselves to bestir him, handed him a bottle of rum and a promise to return the pigs before the master returned. "Is hokay wid me, wunna know. Dem nuh 'tink like brute—hall a dem?"

As the pigs loosened the stumps, the soldiers dug out the remains with pickaxes and shovels. The land began to clear. They took rakes and hoes to it. As the land cleared, it turned black—blackness filled with the richness of the river and the bones of people in unmarked graves. They got a mule and a plow, borrowing them from the same old caretaker; the master was visiting relations in Miami, and the caretaker was happy to be relieved of watering and feeding a mule he no longer drove, which was never fe him anyway.

With the mule and the plow they turned the land over and over. When it was prepared they planted some acres of ganja, and, later, they planted food.

They found, in the process of clearing the land, things that had been planted long before—before even the grandmother—which had managed to survive the density of the wild forest. Cassava. Afu. Fufu. Plantain.

The soldiers left enough forest alive so that they were not visible from the road which passed at the foot of the hill. They lived in a clearing behind a screen. People of course knew someone was there, but they were given to understand only that the granddaughter of Miss Mattie had returned.

The soldiers smoked ganja only occasionally—and then according to strict tradition. But there was a big demand for it in America—where it apparently was used all hours of the day and night—and they traded the dried leaves and seeds to a small-plane pilot, a shaggy whiteman, a man nevertheless with connections, when they met at an airfield cut from bush, near to Endeavour in the Dry Harbour Mountains. This meeting took place every few months. The ammunition and the guns they received for the ganja were passed to them in wooden boxes, stamped MADE IN USA, further information as to their origin broadly stenciled in black on the ends of the boxes: Massachusetts, Virginia, Ohio, Indiana. The pilot explained that this—making weapons—was a big American business. Except he said "Yankee" business, assuming he would not be seen as an enemy but as someone speaking to them on their own terms. He had been a mercenary in Angola; he knew the score.

The yam, cassava, plantain, the coconuts the rats left to them, the perch and crayfish from the river, the Ethiopian apples, all sustained them until their plantings of food began to bear. They filled a kerosene tin with riverwater, added some broken sprigs of wild thyme, fish and yam, cassava and plantain, and boiled up dinner behind their screen each evening. They hollowed out calabashes and dipped their bowls into the soup, and replenished their tiredness. After their meal, they passed the pipe of ganja one by one.

They slept and ate outside, leaving the house to the bats and scorpions and lizards who now possessed it.

The soldiers traded their surplus food, once the plantings were in, for rice, saltfish, coffee, cooking oil, sugar—things they could not produce. The daughter of landowners, dressed in countrywomen's clothes, went to a shop a mile away, at the railway crossing. The tracks were dead, trains had long since stopped running. The shop had sometimes what they needed, sometimes not—people were in the grip of shortages. The woman went on foot with a basket on her head, and bartered surplus food with the owner of the shop, who had arrived in St. Elizabeth from Hong Kong fifty years before.

Slapping her backless black bedroom slippers along the clay road, cutlass in right hand. Basket on head, resting on a cotta, bought years ago in Knightsbridge, a gallery specializing in African art, carried as a talisman. Now being put to use, its true properties recognized. It had not been comfortable on a glass shelf; it belonged on a woman's head. She spoke to the shopkeeper in the name of her grandmother.

The rest of the surplus, all that they could not barter, was distributed by Miss Mattie's granddaughter to people around who did not have enough land to support them. It had been a practice of her mother and grandmother. The woman was used to it—what other use could be made of extra food?

2

NO TELEPHONE
TO HEAVEN

Et ce pays cria pendant des siècles que nous sommes des bêtes brutes; que les pulsations de l'humanité s'arrêtent aux portes de la négrerie; que nous sommes un fumier ambulant hideusement prometteur de cannes tendres et de coton soyeux et l'on nous marquait au fer rouge et nous dormions dans nos excréments et l'on nous vendait sur les places et l'aune de drap anglais et la viande salée d'Irlande coûtaient moins cher que nous, et ce pays était calme, tranquille, disant que l'esprit de Dieu était dans ses actes.

(And this land screamed for centuries that we are bestial brutes; that the human pulse stops at the gates of the slave compound; that we are walking compost hideously promising tender cane and silky cotton and they would brand us with red-hot irons and we would sleep in our excrement and they would sell us on the town square and an ell of English cloth and salted meat from Ireland cost less than we did, and this land was calm, tranquil, repeating that the spirit of the Lord was in its acts.)

—AIMÉ CÉSAIRE,
Cahier d'un Retour au Pays Natal

The truck struggled on up through the Cockpits.

Its side was painted with the motto—in large yellow and red letters outlined in silver metallic, almost faded to nothing by now—NO TELEPHONE TO HEAVEN. The colors and the words an embellishment of the former owner, who had used the vehicle as a means of livelihood, transporting women to the market every Saturday and to church revivals every six months. How these words had come to him they did not know. For his truck they had given him a load of ganja, large enough to hang over the slats in the back, and fixed him up with a connection to get American dollars in exchange. Soon after this transaction, exchanging American dollars for the last natural resource left to them, they heard he had left for England—people were even now leaving for England—where he changed his dollars for pounds and managed to get work as a conductor on an upstairs-bus going through South London and paid some of the ganja money on a little two-up, two-down in Brixton.

NO TELEPHONE TO HEAVEN. No voice to God. A waste to try. Cut off. No way of reaching out or up. Maybe only one way. Not God's way. No matter if him is Jesus or him is Jah. Him not gwan like dis one lickle bit. NO TELEPHONE TO HEAVEN.

The motto suited them. Their people. The place of their people's labor. So lickle movement in this place. From this place. Then only back and forth, back and forth, over and again, over and again—for centuries.

They once all had the belief. Especially the old people. The ones who had handed it to them across scrubbed tables with Sunday rice-and-peas, de watchman atop. The ones in the limestone churches—their bricks sized with molasses. No joke. Sugar nuh strong? The ones under the earth—the conch embellishing the dirt—to the sea nuh mus' return.

The ones in the zinc-roofed Pocomania shacks. Bodies burning in the magnified sun. The ones in the balmyard. But Lord Jesus no balm. During the sacrifices in hidden chapels, bleeding an animal who was not them. Pleading with the faithful zombie. Crawling across the Dungle to a revival tent. Praying to Mother Africa to come save them in Jesus' name. Witnessing in a white tiehead for Jehovah, remembering Shàngó. But him fade. Dressed like poppy-show at a High Anglican mass for the sake of the archbishop-him of Canterbury. Begging Jesus. Jah. Moses. Shàngó. Yemanjá. Oshun. God nuh mus' be deaf.

Some of them worshiped with their bodies. Rum. Ganja. Music. Water. Vision. Fire. Drum. Stone. They lived amid a commotion of rites. Revival Zion. Convince. Ras Mataz. Shouter. Ras Tafari. Pentecostal. Disciples of Christ. Kumina. Furiously at worship. Trying to make communion with God Almighty. No matter what him name be. What her name be.

Sasabonsam. Marley. Mighty Sparrow. Garvey. Nanny. Rhyging.

Hear me, Myal-man. Hear me, Obeah-man. Hear me, Jumby-man. Dem say you is magical.

Rum. Ganja. Mento. Ska. Reggae. Prayer. Singing. Jump-up. Hymns. Full-immersion baptism. Nine Night.

Nigromancy.

Early death for so many. But no relief. Many of them is sufferah. Many of them live in Passion. Suffering nuh mus' be meant for we.

Depression. Downpression. Oppression. Recession. Intercession. Commission. Omission. Missionaries.

Is nuh dry-jump dis.

All the same t'ing, mi dear. We is in Babylon. Yes, mi dear bredda. NO TELEPHONE TO HEAVEN.

Maybe the line it is engaged and God can't bodder wid de likes of we. God nuh mus' be Hinglish. But me did 'ear once dat Jesus-him did 'ave bad 'air. Mus' be one joke 'pon we.

Sucking their teeth. Throwing words at the moon. Per-'aps the line to heaven is one party line. No telling who will answer or who will be listening in. Taking down our names. How long mus' we wait to get t'rough? We have been royally deceived. Who God like? Not we. NO TELEPHONE TO HEAVEN.

But how could Massa God be their enemy? The sea-water which hid their history was not at fault. The moon which lit the sea. The sun which warmed the swallowtail to flight. The flicker of the click beetle. The charge of the mad ant. The breath of the coral reef. The gray shark. The blue mountains. The black widow. The brown widow. The thick stands of Black Mangrove.

None of these were the enemy.

They were tired of praying for those that persecuted them.

Guns were not strangers to them. Tivoli Gardens and Red Hills had run with their blood. Staining the cement-block walls some of them had set in place, some of them had washed white or painted mango yellow or tropic green. Spilling into cesspools some of them had dug. Poor t'ings.

They hadn't been prepared to be used so. They had been called gardenboys houseboys countryboys. They had called themselves cowboys spreeboys rudeboys. Let de gal mind de pickney, me is free. Is gal job dat. God nuh say so? God again.

In the seventies they entered the territory of the opposition, their own party's line held tight in their heads. They entered the territory of the opposition with guns and rocks and Red Stripe bottles with flaming tops, filled with kerosene. They called themselves po-lict-ti-cal men. They said they had mighty leaders they trusted. One called himself Joshua, who would lead them from the wilderness.

How him could know the wilderness would be so difficult to cross.

They fired missiles at each other. They bled. NO TELEPHONE TO HEAVEN.

And some of their mothers and sisters, applying cleaning fluids to the fake-tudor homes of Toronto or fighting the teenager roaches in the high-rise condominiums of New York, saw the reports on CBC or CBS that Jamaica was about to hexplode. Tourism was suffering. Vacationers were endangered. The stench of burning Michelins cut into the night. The mother or the sister try to reach home.

NO TELEPHONE TO HEAVEN. Lord Jesus, dem fighting amongst demselves as usual. The mother or the sister is embarrassed if the mistress catch her watching the television while she iron or cook or clean or pick up after de white pickney dem. The mother or the sister is shamed if the mistress stop and glance at the television as well, glance at she homeland, she people, a small smile or thin look of concern on the mistress face, forgetting, or remembering, to whom she is speaking, and saying, "Well, I guess that's another place they've ruined for us."

The eyes of the mother or the sister turn down. And the shame on behalf of her people—Lord Jesus, hear me nuh, why dem cyaan behave demselves. Dem nuh wuthless?—gives way to fury, precious fury, and the eyes remain downcast for the mistress might catch the fire. What de blasted hell dat blood-clat bitch know 'bout hit? Licklemos' she draw me in. But me stop me tongue because of lickle monies—and me no have de green cyard. Hif me can stan' she husband panting and blowing down me face, me can tek she hinsult.

And the mother or the sister withdraws to her lickle room, resting her legs on a cardboard box covered with pretty paper, worrying that her homeland and her people will burn.

NO TELEPHONE TO HEAVEN. Fighting among themselves—as usual. How did they come to this?

Was this so bad? At least they were doing something. At least they were not sitting on some mountainside smoking ganja and waiting on Jah. They were not dressed in white shirts and black pants standing at attention on a hotel verandah waiting for some tourist's order. Lounging at a rumshop. Begging at the racetrack. At least they were not dressed in khaki sitting in a small and dark back room listening to Rediffusion, waiting for the mistress to return home to say what shrubs needed trimming or what flower she want cut fe de table. A man could be kept waiting for hours on end, and the mistress, or the master, or the son, or the daughter, or the relative who lodged with them would never even think to say, "Sorry, Winston, to waste your afternoon so." That was the worst of being a servant. The waiting around for cuffy-pretend-backra or backra-fe-true while your life passed, the people in the house assuming your time was worthless. Assuming you could not judge the beauty of a ginger blossom or arrange roses of peace in a cut-glass vase.

If you were a man who worked in the house, who waited on the dining table, you had to listen while the master or the mistress or the lickle master or the lickle mistress or the unmarried auntie who lived with them talked about their day, or the *Gleaner,* or the cost of gas, or the price of rice, or their opinion that there were by now far too many cars in Kingston, or what kind of mess is Manley trying to make of Jamaica, how him can surround himself wid such ruffians, they ask, never realizing a ruffian is serving them dinner, or realizing it all the while but wanting to let the ruffian know that he is to be kept in this dining room come hell or high water. Come Armageddon to Babylon.

One night, the man who serves the table, who attends meetings on his evenings off, unable to hold his tongue any longer, turns to the people at the table, and says, "You know, Mas' William, when we get de power, de power fe de people, t'ings not gwan be easy fe de white smaddy of Jamaica dem. Per'haps wunna and wunna family should t'ink 'bout de hemigration. Wit' all respect, sah."

"I never did hear such rudeness, Faith." The master speaks across the server to the mistress.

"We are not white, Joshua, so we are not worried." The mistress taking pity on the houseboy and deciding that his words came from benign concern. Flattered nonetheless that even this hignorant countrybwai did t'ink she white. Not understanding his use of metaphor.

"So you say, missis. Wunna t'roat may still be cut." The man who serves the table addresses himself softly; no one asks him to repeat his words. He addresses himself as he backs out of the room with a tray of rice and green gunga and roast pork. He will store it in the refrigerator before he takes his own dinner of *bacalao* and white yam.

NO TELEPHONE TO HEAVEN. Indeed. As Paul H. found out. Returning home to Stony Hill one Sunday morning after an all-night party at Buster Said's house. A holiday brukins in the seventies. Pool and champagne and live band and true wildness. The mother and father in Ocho Rios for the weekend. Buster naked in the pool comparing cocks with his cousin Pedro from Caracas. "We nuh is outstanding cocksmen, bra." Dancing in the chlorinated water arm in arm. Background music. To Be Young, Gifted, and Black finally come to Ja. Reggae-style. Number one on Rediffusion and JBC. Drinking the Piper-Heidsieck Buster's father got from the cellar in one of his three hotels. Someone asks the band to switch from reggae to something else. "Lawks, man, every blasted maid in Kingston singing that song." "Hey, Jude." La la la la. la-la-la-la. la-la-la-la. "Hey, Jude." Better. No, man, too previous. Some girl throwing up into the deep end of the pool. Someone's overseas cousin pale from compulsive intermarriage and northern lights come back for the Christmas not used to the sun and the food and too much champagne. At the bar, by the shallow end, someone adds rum to a glass of champagne, regards the glass as the paleness turns to gold, and calls it "Planter's Pickney." Pedro has brought mescal with him and cheerfully offers it around. Then Harry/Harriet, boy-girl, Buster's brother-sister, half–brother-sister actually, who was always strange, since childhood, they say, but everyone tolerates him, as if measuring their normalness against his strangeness. He is *only* one, after all, one that nature did not claim. He is vastly outnumbered, will—unless they protect him, because he is also one of them, though apart from them, reminding them of their wholeness—he will end up in some back-o'-wall alley in Raetown, fucked to death. Him cyaan help himself, him mother nuh maid? Harry/Harriet puts on a bikini—bra stretched across his hairy, delicately mounded chest, panties cradling his cock and balls—and starts to dance to "Hey, Jude." People laugh but nobody takes Harry/Harriet to heart. "You won't laugh so when I am appearing in London with the Royal Ballet and the Queen come fe see me." Laughs and more laughs. "I shall be at Cable Hut tomorrow, dancing with the sun behind me." Pause. "Come if you want some pussy." "Lord, Harry, where you get pussy?" "You would be surprised, massa." They kill off the champagne and then start in on the ganja, chasing it with the rest of the rum. John D., who dreds his hair and whose daddy teaches African studies at the university, has brought the ganja with him. He quite seriously denounces rum as an "imperialist" drink. "Lef' it wid de touris', man. Have some talawa smoke. Is Rasta grass dis. Pure Jamaican gold. Lamb's bread, bredda. Rum come from cane. Drink rum you is marked like Cain. Smoke lamb's bread you is lamb of Jah. Drink rum become like touris'. Tourism is whorism, bredda. You want to favor whore of Babylon?" The band, interrupting before the itation takes flight, suddenly switches to calypso, with an ease born of steady North Coast gigs. Next t'ing they going to limbo and pass their red-jacketed selves under a firestick. "Take me to Jamaica where the rum come from, the rum come from, the rum come from/Take me to Jamaica where the rum come from/And we will have some fun." John D. wanders off and watches a shooting star from under a bank of bougainvillea. "Man," say Buster, "that not calypso, that collapse-so. Lef' it to Byron Lee and the Dragonaires dem." There is some kind of action in the poolhouse, where Buster has provided air mattresses. One boy, the one they call Cricket Ball because of the smooth roundness of his head, removes a gun from his shoulder holster when the girl underneath say it jook her. Him pass it to two boys, blood brothers, sitting in a corner, who are discussing the gold market in London where they are studying to be brokers. They fiddle with the gun and talk about Fidel and how we need guns so that what happen to them don't happen to us. Cricket Ball raises his head. "Man, you cyaan talk somewhere else? Don't you have *no* sensitivity?"

At about 6 A.M., Paul H. leaves behind the shambles of the party, unconcerned about the mess. He has never been concerned about a mess in his life. He and his surroundings have been tidied by darker people. He gets into his Porsche and drives farther up into the hills. He lives with his family, as most well-off Jamaicans do until they get married, or leave the island. The winding road, lit with the early morning sun, offers little resistance to the Porsche. The road takes Paul past numerous large stucco and tiled-roof houses, set back in pastel shades, with iron gates and large dogs chained or roaming across the carefully trimmed and planted grounds.

Denizens caught in dream behind narrow louvers or iron-mongered pineapples, masked barriers.

It was quiet that morning when Paul arrived home to Stony Hill. Turning his head, all of Kingston was below him, the harbor and airport clearly visible, an Avianca jet gliding silently from Quito down into Palisadoes. He got out of the Porsche and the bright sun played hell with his head. He unlocked the gate and looked around for Carlos, the Great Dane, surprised that the dog hadn't barked when he approached. He whistled. Nothing. Then he spied Carlos lying under a hedge of white poinsettia, and wondered further at the dog's silence when he called his name until his eyes met with Carlos' neck and Paul saw the thick red line of a wound from ear to ear. Machete.

An intruder. But his father had guns in the house and even now he knew that the family was asleep, having driven off the intruder. Obviously they hadn't found Carlos in the dark when the intruder must have entered. He would have to break the news gently to his sister, to whom Carlos really belonged and who probably had gone to sleep hoping the dog had run off in the confusion. He took a few dried fronds from the base of a Jamaican tall and covered the dog. He would bury him later, after taking a shower and clearing his head and getting a few hours' sleep before the rest of the family awoke and wanted to tell him about the incident of the night. And whether his father had made contact with the flesh of the man foolish enough to disturb them. Things were getting truly out of hand, his father would say. And his mother would wonder whether Miami was such a bad place. His father would respond that the day has yet to dawn that will see him leave his island to them.

Paul got back in the Porsche and drove up to the garage, parked, and began to walk toward the house. It was so quiet. Only the waking-up of birds and a soft breeze from the sea through the trees around the house sounded any-

thing. But when he got to the verandah his command of
certainty began to give way. There was a strange sweet smell
to the clean morning air. It was familiar, but he could not
place it. A fly buzzed past his ear and, when he swatted at
it, fell, suddenly, with a flat sound, plopping onto the pink
speckled tiles of the verandah. He stepped on it without
really thinking and thick dark blood spread from its body
onto the porch floor and stained the instep of one of his
white loafers. Perhaps it had fed on Carlos, he thought. Not
wondering why the fly had appeared on the verandah. Soon
there was another fly; Paul let it be. He reached into his
pocket for his keys and, when he went to unlock it, noticed
that the dark, heavy mahogany door—cut with naïve scenes
of the old days, bought by his father at an estate auction in
Warsop—the door was slightly open. Something happened
to his insides at that instant. The keys to the door—its an-
tiquity had been disturbed to carve holes and place three
dead bolts—the keys to the door hung useless in his left
hand. He was without hope. The thing that happened to
other people had happened to him. An open door could
signify but one reality at that hour on that hot morning in
that sloping yard in that well-kept part of the city. He walked
forward into his family's house.

Nothing had been disturbed in the living room or the
dining room. Except for the abundance of flies lighting here
and there, all seemed normal, untouched—the table prepared for Sunday morning breakfast, white linen rectangles
protecting each place-setting. He walked into the kitchen,
knowing the end of his journey would be the bedrooms but
desperate to wait, until the tide of his sweat calmed, until
he woke to find his conclusion undone, until the dream rav-
eled suddenly, as he slept.

Someone had made bacon and eggs; the iron frying pan
was on the stove, a white crust of egg swimming in bacon
fat. Paul put his finger in the fat; it was warm. The larder
off the kitchen, locked by his mother each evening, unlocked by her each time the maid had need of something,

was opened wide. Someone had made havoc with the carefully stored contents of the shelves. His mother's order. Broken bottles of Pickapeppa and Tia Maria dripped their contents, the dark liquids mingling on the floor. Bags of rice, precious import, ripped at the seams, spilled forth, and the grains now crunched under his feet. Tins of wet sugar and tins of Milo had rolled into recesses under the shelves, dented where they bounced and came to rest. Salt, thyme, coffee, ginger root, pepper, curry powder, onions, gunga peas, red beans, bacalao, black-eye peas—all the ingredients of Jamaica were mixed together in this mess.

In the middle of the kitchen, a plate, in pieces on the floor, showed on a few fragments more traces of egg, dried and hard. As a final touch, an almost inevitable highlight to the chaos, a stream of urine ran down a far wall and puddled in the middle of the kitchen around the shards of china.

He turned and left the room, making his way to the long hall off the family room, which ended in the bedrooms. Flies were swarming all up and down the hall. Everywhere. He stopped and watched some come through the aluminum louvers and watched others fly from another direction and navigate into walls. These, he reasoned, as if the habits of flies should be his concern, these were the filled and drunken ones, confused revelers, unable to find a way out. They hit the white and softly colored walls around him, specking them wildly, and then dropped to the straw runner, like fat old men who had been celebrating the Christmas, now dozing into Sunday, sleeping it off. A ghostly croaker slid from under a closet door and trapped one on his sticky tongue.

Paul turned into his parents' room, the wide master bedroom, carpeted wall-to-wall in pale yellow. The louvers at the far end were cracked open, and sunlight slid into the room and enlightened the people in the bed. The sunlight dancing across what had taken place in the still of the night. Playing shades of hibiscus across his father.

His father, it seemed to Paul, had put up no struggle. He lay on his back, naked and barehanded, his pajama top on the floor at least five yards away, his trousers not to be seen. His throat was cut like the dog's throat was cut, and his penis was severed, so that it hung from his crotch as if on a thin string, dangling into the place between his open legs. How could he not defend himself? His wife? His eyes were closed—they told nothing.

The room stirred around Paul as if there were life in it. Not his alone, not the dancing sun and flower shadows, not the vivacity of the flies which made a thick black line under his father's chin and gathered at his seed. The stirring felt like an aftershock. Duppy? No, man. The room stilled. The son stirred within. He who believed and could not yet truly believe. Bredda, you is one royal fool. But how it can be so?

He heaved, caught his breath, and walked around the bottom of the king-sized bed to his mother's side. She was also uncovered. Naked, as his father was naked, but with one arm across her eyes as if protecting herself from the eyes of others. Her nature. Did she wonder who would find her? Had she spent her last instant in this life thinking about it? He moved to touch her face, gently. Afraid even now that she would wake and be angry that he had seen her so. Bwai, you facey. Hoping against hope for her anger. Afraid of her. Even his gentle touch to her cool face created chaos, as the back of her head sank deep into her pillow, widening the gap in her throat. His throat caught. He looked down at her, away from her neck, to where he had emerged twenty-five years before. The base of a rum bottle was caught between her legs. Wha' fe do? Terror at approaching this part of her. Have mercy. He pulled the bottle out and saw that the neck was broken. Jagged. Blood poured from between her legs, catching in her fine curled hair. The flies swarmed anew as a new banquet lay before them. He felt a terrible shame.

The smell rose higher in the room as the sun rose higher and invaded with greater brightness. It seemed the room was baking. He lost control. He vomited on the floor beside his mother, burning his throat. He got up, head filled now with dizziness, and walked into their bathroom. Washed his hands and face with cold water and spat into the sink. He splashed bay rum over his face and hands, trying to get the smell from his nostrils. He left to find his sister.

He found her as he dreaded, in her youth bed with its thin rail. Her legs were spread wide and she was bloodied. The gold bangle on her wrist glinted in the light. *Beast,* came into his spinning head.

And still he did not weep. He sat on a chair in a corner of her room and put his head in his hands and tried to think of what to do. How to get rid of all of this. He needed help.

He thought of Christopher, who sometimes tended the yard for them. Yes. Paul would call him at his girlfriend's house where he lodged now and again. Yes. He would ask Christopher to come and help him clean up the mess, offering him a few dollars for his trouble. And maybe after, he would tell him, they could go to bush to shoot some birds. It did not occur to Paul to call the police for anything at all. The police were worthless. These things happened. Things were out of hand. The police would pick up some laborer, some aimless soul, and let it go at that.

Paul would have Christopher come; they would clean the house, remove the bodies, and carry them down to country where his father's unmarried sister still lived. He would bury them on the family property. He would tele-graph ahead to the local preacher and ask him to tell the auntie to have the ground prepared. The ground would be burned and opened. The preacher would say a few words over the family and that would be that. It was only in the process of making these plans, in thinking of cleaning up the house, disposing of the remains, that he remembered Mavis. It had not come into his mind until now that Mavis had not gone out the evening before, and it was his duty to look into her room to see if she was there. He picked himself up from the chair in his sister's room and went back through the house to the small room at the side of the garage.

Her body was on the floor, slashed in a way none of his family had been slashed. The machete had been dug into her in so many ways, so many times, that Mavis' body became more red than brown. She had no more eyes.

Paul was faced with a problem upon this discovery. They did not know, he did not know, how to reach Mavis' people. He did not know her surname, or the name of the place she had come from. She appeared at the gate about five years before looking for work, just come from down a country. His mother might have known, for she had hired her, but there would be no canceled checks to reveal a surname, because Mavis was paid in cash each week, and each week his father complained to his mother about the amount. That was all Paul knew, except that wherever she came from, she had, like most maids, a couple of children she sent her money to. He opened the one drawer of the dresser in her room: panties, a small bottle of smelling salts, brassieres, folded cotton cloths—that was all. On top of the dresser was Mavis' Bible and her lime-green plastic purse. He opened the purse to find a couple of dollars and some change, nothing else. He flipped through the Bible, but no family record appeared. No papers. No birth certificate. No savings book, no insurance policy. No verses were underscored. No letters pressed between the thin leaves. He was truly stupid if he thought he would find anything from the contents of this room which would reveal this woman's name, the names of her ancestors, the name of her mother, her father, her place of birth, her date of birth, the names and ages of her children. Her opinion of life. It was not his fault; it was hopeless. He could not bury her in the family plot—his auntie would never allow it. He would just have to burn her body along with the sheets and nightclothes and pillows stained with blood. He had no sadness left for anyone but himself. He was sorry, but that was just the situation in which he

28

found himself. He felt *inconvenience* at the presence of Mavis' body and found himself turning on her in his head. Was the *beast* some man she dragged back from a dance? No. No, Mavis had stayed in that evening. He remembered.

Paul left the maid's room and returned to the living room. He reached Christopher's girlfriend by telephone, after being asked sharply by her mumma what him business wid she daughter. He knew the girl's name and number because he used Christopher to carry his guns when he went bird-shooting and picked him up in the Porsche on the way to the blind. "Some kind of cyar dis, eh, bwai?" "Yes, sah."

He reached the girl. She told him that Christopher had not been with her that night and that if Mas' Paul see him, him to tell de bwai she damn vex'. Is jus' who him t'ink him is? Fockin' Shaft? Paul hung up the phone and went out onto the verandah. At that instant he saw Christopher strolling up the driveway. Paul ran to meet him in a sudden, as he had run to meet him when they were boys. Suddenly filled with relief; no longer alone in all this.

"Man, Lord, man, I glad to see you. It terrible, man . . . somet'ing terrible happen inside, bredda. Dem dead . . . hall a dem . . . chopped to rass . . ."

"Who done hit?"

"Me nuh know, man . . . nuh some wuthless bastard . . . some damn beas' kill hall a dem." His voice started to crack. He stopped speaking.

"Lord Jesus. Lord Jesus, Mas' Paul." Christopher lowered his eyes.

For a time they just stood, Paul fighting emotion. Surviving by changing the subject.

"Me call your gal fe try fe reach you. She say to tell you she vex' wid you. Soun' like she tu'n one true virago, man."

"Rass, man," Christopher sucked his teeth. "Rass. Hit no Satiday night las' night, Mas' Paul? Jus' a lickle rum. Lickle Chrismus spree."

Paul nodded.

Christopher carried with him, as he always did, being a casual laborer, his machete. Sharp and clean. Many young men seeking work for an hour or two could be seen walking through the streets of the city's richer suburbs in khaki, tool hanging loosely from their hands. As Christopher stood in front of Paul he cradled his machete across his chest, like the young man with a horn.

"You wan' mek a few dollar?" No more talk of what had been done, Paul spoke of wha' fe do.

"Sah?"

"Help me clean up de house, and come wid me to country to bury de body dem." His tone was even.

"Okay, bredda." Christopher paused. "But, Mas' Paul, wunna not gwan phone fe de police?"

"Nuh, man. Dem wuthless. Whosoever done dis is long gone."

"What wunna wan' me fe do?"

"Mek one fire in de back. We have fe bu'n de sheets and other t'ings dem."

"Hokay."

"Mek me go telegraph a country to say we come."

Paul left Christopher in the yard and went back into the house.

Christopher had stopped by the house about two that morning. Went directly into Mavis room to tell she him hongry and beg she fetch him sinting to eat. She complain and she fret the master will wake. But she go to the kitchen for him. She tell him to wait in her room and she will bring back food fe him. Saltfish and ackee left over from her dinner, the only real food in the refrigerator, she say, not telling him about the bacon and eggs for the family's Sunday breakfast. Him hab no business wid such food. No. She told him the fridge contained oranges, condensed milk, some opened bottles of condiments, and the leftover saltfish and ackee—all else was locked in the larder, or hard like one rockstone in the freezer.

As she stood by the stove warming the snack for Christopher, he entered the kitchen behind her, bumping up against her so she could smell the rum on his breath. "Lawd, man, why you cyaan wait in me room like me ask?" She sucked her teeth, but did it softly; if the master catch she is hell she gwan pay. Fixing food fe one yardbwai in de people kitchen when dem sleep. "Lawd, man, go wait in me room and me will bring de food. . . . Hear me, nuh?"

"No, missis. Me hab business wid Mas' Charles. Me have fe talk wid him. Food can wait." Christopher swayed in the dim kitchen. Mavis did not light the big light; it seemed to her the master could smell a bulb burning, even when him fas' asleep.

"What wunna could have fe talk wid him about . . . ? Bwai, hear me! Hit cyaan wait till mornin'?" The bwai was stubborn. Black-up and stubborn.

She let him pass her by. It was his own lookout. She put away the pan and replaced the leftovers in the fridge, shut off the small light, and went back to her own room, cursing the bwai's wuthlessness as she found her way.

They were fast asleep. In their big bedroom. Sleeping deeply—what his grandmother would have called the sleep of the righteous, which she always promised him for being a good boy. She had little else to promise him.

The two of them had lived in a lickle shack in a shantytown near the Esso refinery on the outskirts of Kingston. A town of structures built by women and children. Structures made from packing crates which once housed Vauxhalls, Morris Minors, Renaults, Kelvinators, Frigidaires, Maytag washer-dryers. Found by a woman after an overseas shipment came in, discarded behind one of the big dealers downtown. Dragged by the woman and her children through the streets of Kingston, where they were noticed and commented upon. Structures made more commonly—for a packing crate was a true luxury, a blessed discovery—from bits and pieces, findings. Structures crowned with sheets of zinc, the places where the zinc rusted filled with cardboard or newspaper or left to gape. Structures made from lengths of corrugated paper, sheets of corrugated metal. Some enhanced by colored metal signs in places, used as patches, advertising Dragon Stout, Four Aces Cigarettes, Golden Guinea Soap, the People's National Party. But most were not so picturesque—most relied on the *Gleaner* or the *Star* to interrupt the blank flatness of the building materials.

Women and children jammed together with other women and children, and a few old men, discarded elders, scattered about. Shacks clustered around a standpipe which dripped into the ground. The force of the water when turned on hardly more than the dripping. Women on line with their enamel pans, filled with old condensed milk tins used as cups, flattened tins used as plates, all manner of scarred utensils. The place-settings of scavengers.

This was the Dungle. Here was the dung-heap jungle where people squirmed across mountains of garbage. On one mountainside stood their home. The Dungle perimetered by a seven-foot-high fence of uneven and rusty zinc wall, one entry and one exit.

Children with swirls of white ringworm interrupting their brown skin, raised lines moving outward into circles, exploding here and there, spreading. Inside these same children worms attached themselves with hooks, thin pale ribbons sending segments of themselves outside the child, to be found squirming in the cracked white chamberpots, where the dogs drank, or among the gray acacia shrubs, where the children squatted. The makka-thorned acacia. The bush from which the Ark was carved and the Crown was woven. So dem say. Jamakka. The only bush alive in the Dungle. The thorns drawn into the children, into their feet and hands, their slender buttocks.

The bones of these children, their legs and arms, bent into bows, and could not grow easily. They were small, all of them—except for their rounded bellies, which pained them in emptiness. Uptown, begging work, a woman had seen the

32

pictures of a Biafra baby posted outside a big Anglican church, along with a plea for donations. She had to laugh.

Most of the children of the Dungle did not go to school, and so few could read. It was only from the pictures on the signs around them that they could tell what was being advertised on the walls of the shacks—evidences of the world outside. A glass of dark liquid with a creamy foam; a dark woman in a tiehead, smiling; the black and red symbols of spades, clubs, diamonds, hearts; a light-skinned elderly man with his mouth open. Stout, soap, cigarettes, politics. Politricks, rastaman say.

The children played in the ground around the shacks, tunneled into the mountainsides, watched after their mothers' other babies while the women walked the city looking for food or begging work. Hunting through the trash behind the big hotels. Diving into a heavy steel drum, they came up with all manner of sinting. A slice of fruit from someone's planter's punch. Pieces of green banana or chocho, cut into scalloped or zigzagged edges, a garnish from a stranger's lobster, caught at Lime Cay that very morning. Remains of food prepared for the visitors, flown in, packed in ice on silver jets, unfamiliar—like the carcasses of roast turkey which appeared each afternoon dumped from the luncheon buffet at Myrtle Bank. The white meat sliced away, but nice bits on the back and thighs. Would be like de Chrismus wid dis—could mek soup wid hit—jus' fill one pan from de pipe an' bil' one fiah houtside. Or she might spy the splintered bones of curried goat, sucked clean, which some businessman had at lunch, sharing nostalgia for a country upbringing with a contact. These were dangerous and could draw her blood should she touch them suddenly.

As she searched, she fought the streetdogs, the scrawny, lonely presences of the city—diving deep, the mother would take whatever she grasped. These things went into a crocus sack which she rested on her hip, tightly protecting it against the dogs which followed her, even the ones whose teats hung slack and empty. Against other women who might have found nothing. Against the black-up men leaning against the city-walls telling her dey sweet 'pon she an' wan' fe grease de crease. She carried her bag of remains on her hip and looked straight ahead.

Her raids into the discarded bounty of the hotels had to be made almost silently because there was always some-one eager to catch her, tell her she was wuthless, drive her off. Tell her she too ugly, too stink to scour dem nastiness.

More often than not the turkey bones remained a dream of hers. More often than not she returned empty-handed, her head bent into her slack chest. More often than not she was too tired to begin her search, and her children scoured the hills of the Dungle.

Christopher lived in this heaped-up settlement with his grandmother until he was eight; when she died, he remained for two more years.

In a shack with walls of thin gray wood barely able to support a roof of zinc, an interior collage of *Gleaner* and *Star* headlines, a picture of Our Saviour, a photograph of Alexander Bustamante. One iron cot on which his grand-mother slept; when she died he moved into it. A piece of scrubbed board on the floor on which they ate. A chipped enamel ewer containing water and a smooth thunderstone, maintaining the health of the water. A firewall. A hole in the roof above the firewall. A cardboard box in one corner, turned upwards, where his grandmother rested her Bible, the letters J. Wray & Nephew Ltd. visible on the box. In the Bible, his grandmother had printed her name, her daughter's name, her grandson's name. When her daughter left, when his mother took off one day, when a dark wom-an's body was washed up on the shore outside a badhouse in Raetown, his grandmother took a piece of charred wood from the fire where she simmered a soup of banana skins and wild callaloo begged from a higgler in Trench Town and with it drew a thick line through the name of her daughter.

Their picture of Our Saviour would have surprised most people. It showed a small dark man with a hump on his back—a gift from the pastor of the Church of the Lickle Jesus, Brother Josephus.

In his faith the brother combed the Dungle, searching for souls to bring to Lickle Jesus. Carrying a sign painted with his idea of Jesus, the pastor trudged across the garbage, saying, "Brother, Sister, gather to me . . . mek me show you my lickle Jesus . . . mek me tell of what Him do . . . mek me tell you, children, how Him is like we . . . how the Son of Massa God favor we . . . how the Word speak to we . . . in Jesus' name, beg you hear me!

"Brother, Sister, gather to me. . . ."

After each passage across the hills of the stinking Dungle, filth stuck to his hard bare feet, Brother Josephus would return to the one-room cement-block structure which was his church and wash his feet in a tin basin filled from the standpipe in the yard he shared with a card-player and a dressmaker and a man who played the mouth organ day and night. Into the basin the pastor scattered dried rose petals. Red petals bought from an Indian merchant, dyed with the blood of Lickle Jesus floating in the dingy citywater. So the brother thought. So the brother taught. Lickle Jesus was in his every vision. Lickle Jesus was his company. The rose petals weighted with sadness sinking under the surface of the dark water. As his traveled feet rested in the petaled water, the brother shut his eyes and watched as the Magdalene dried the feet of Lickle Jesus with her hair. Dredlocks which by the grace of Our Heavenly Father covered her nakedness.

One Sunday morning when Christopher was about seven, he and his grandmother entered the church and sat on the bench in the back. About ten people clustered in the church—ten people plus the grandmother and the grandson surrounded by walls painted red and gold and purple, black lines running through the color, lines curling into images and symbols, and letters from some unknown alphabet. Incense burned in this place strange to them. Smoking sticks stood in scrubbed cobalt bottles which once held remedies.

35

The scented tendrils of sandalwood haloed the brother and reached among the congregants. They found themselves in a place of sudden images and sweet smells. Things they were unused to. Things they did not trust.

The brother broke a flat cassava bammy into pieces and poured some Wincarnis tonic wine into a calabash carved with flying fish. He set these on the altar behind him and spoke to his flock. The eyes of the children lit on the offering of food.

"And the real Jesus . . . the true Jesus . . . the Jesus who come to us is one of us. Look 'pon him countenance, my children! Look 'pon the likeness of the Son of God!" He swept his hand upward, and turned to point to the cloth hanging above the altar. A piece of crocus sack with Christ made in charcoal. Rude. The profile of a small dark man with wooly hair, beardless face, and a hump between his shoulder blades. "Dis, children . . . dis, children, is Lickle Jesus. Black as his mother was Black. As the world came from the darkness of his Father." Brother Josephus bowed his head. "Lickle Jesus, help my flock here so find demselves in you. Teach dem dat even de least of we is you."

A few of the congregants nodded, from politeness more than assent; others sat stone still, the apparent delusion of the brother passing through their minds. How him can say Jesus Black? Cyaan be so. Could be?

"Now . . . there will be those amongst you who will doubt . . . who will not believe what I say to you—"

Brother Josephus was interrupted by a woman in front, her head tied in white cloth, her spectacles reflecting Lickle Jesus.

"Wid all respect, bredda. Me have seen Jesus. Me know is who Him favor."

"Tell me, sister, is how you know?" the brother challenged her gently.

"Teacher nuh show me when we lickle children? Him is backra man fe true. White-white wid blue yeye." She paused, turning her head to face the congregation. "Dat picture dere favor slave, not Saviour." She sucked her teeth, then turned again to meet the brother's eyes. "Mine you don't talk blasphemy, bredda. Mine you'self. Is one mare's nest . . . all a dis . . . one piece of bunga foolishness."

Brother Josephus tried to summon a booming voice which would sway her and convince the other congregants she and they had been deceived. "You tell me, missis, tell me where it say in de Bible Jesus white." Oh, Lickle Jesus, why dem cyaan see you like I see you? Why dem cyaan find demselves in de mystery of you?

The woman did not respond directly. She stood, gathered her fan and Bible, smoothed her skirt, held tight to her purse, and walked out into the morning light away from the dark brother's mischief.

Inside, relieved that others had not joined her, the brother tried to recapture his flock. "It no say nowhere in the teachings of Almighty God dat Jesus white. Nowhere a-tall, a-tall. I say to you, Jesus was as Black as dat bwai dere." Indicating with his left hand, he summoned Christopher to rise. "What you name, bwai?" He had no idea, yet he was drawn to this boy, the darkest of the three in the room.

"Christopher, sah."

A gift for the brother. God sent this child to him. He would get the flock back. He spoke with an urgency, rushing, an excitement flooding his voice. "So . . . so. So it is . . . now and ever shall be. And . . . you name come from the ancient tongue of the Greek . . . you know what you name signify?"

"No, sah."

"Is one talawa name, bwai. One talawa name. A name which possess magic. You is one lucky bwai to have such a name. It mean . . . you name mean the bearer of Christ. Children, dis here bwai is name' bearer of Christ . . . him who bring Lickle Jesus into de New World. Into our world. T'ink 'pon dese t'ings. Christ come wid Columbus. Christ come wid de Christophine . . . what some island people call de cho-cho. Is de fruit of Lickle Jesus. Consider

37

dat . . . consider, children, de lips of de Christophine. How dem split like woman. Is de mother of Lickle Jesus dat."

A woman rose and left.

"Consider . . . consider . . . the flat green seed of . . . the flat green seed dat is within the fruit. Is de seed of God. De seed from which Lickle Jesus grow.

"Christopher . . . Christophine . . . is all the same . . . is a magical name. Dem bring we Jesus . . . nuh mus' be so? Yes. And Lickle Jesus—" He shut his eyes and his eyelids twitched as if his vision fought him. "Lickle Jesus come wid Christophe. Tell me, children, who amongst you can talk of the life of Christophe?"

People were restless under the zinc against sun. Sweat beaded their faces. No one responded to the brother's request, whether out of ignorance, or fear.

"Mek me tell you . . . mek me save you from your ignorance. Mek me tell you of dis Black man who carry Christ amongst de Black people of Haiti. Christophe was de pure Black man who lead de Black people of Haiti dem against de mixed-up ones who want fe control de Africans dem. Jus' like ya so in Jamaica. Christophe know, for Lickle Jesus tell him, him know well dat de ones who mixed, de ones who talk 'my white grandmother' or 'my English father'—dese ones carry Satan in dem blood. Jus' so . . . jus' like dem would carry typhoid . . . cancer . . . for it eat at dem. Dem cyaan help demselves, but dem is tainted. Jus' like in Jamaica. Is because you under dem control dat you cyaan see Jesus as him is.

"But Bredda Christophe bear Lickle Jesus in him heart. And Toussaint, Bredda All-Saint, him know fe we Jesus too. . . . Bredda All-Saint him smash de craven image in de whiteman church. Yes, my children, Toussaint tek de white marble sinting and smash it because it no show Jesus . . . de Jesus Christophe carry in him breast . . . de true everlasting Christ."

The brother paused, sighed heavily.

"T'ink of dis bwai name' Christopher. Tu'n to de side,

bwai." Christopher did as he was told. "See him back? See how him resemble Lickle Jesus? Dis is my body which is broken fe you." Brother Josephus pointed where Christopher's spine was curved from the Dungle. "Him nuh favor Lickle Jesus? Him is true bredda of Lickle Jesus. Him have Christ in him heart. Him is Christlike. Christ like him. Mek we pray."

The majority of the congregants were unconvinced.

When the service was over, Brother Josephus felt a sadness overtake him, as a sadness overtook him after each preachment, as person after person rejected the identification he offered them. As the congregants rushed and muttered their way out, he made a sign for Christopher to stay. The brother turned and picked up a small container from the altar cloth. "Dis here, bwai, hold de chrism. Wid dis mek me anoint you." Christopher bowed his head. The smell of the ointment was sweet, coconut oil mingling with laurel and almond. With delicate fingers, Brother Josephus applied the ointment to the sides of Christopher's head, his forehead, his lips. "Now, bwai, you are blessed as Christ-bearer."

Brother Josephus took down the icon of Christ and handed it to the boy. "Fe you, bwai . . . tek dis wid you. . . . Remember, dis is the face and body of Jesus, and him favor you."

Christopher took the gift without looking up at the brother. "T'ank you, sah."

Outside, his grandmother and another congregant assured passersby that the man was stark raving mad and they should not set foot inside his cement-block church. "Him t'ink him is prophet. Him is heresy himself."

Christopher emerged from the building, the crocus sack held under his arm.

"Bwai, why you smell so?"

But his grandmother let Christopher put the crocus-sack picture into place in their collage where the smoke from the firewall further darkened the image of Christ. The boy held it dear and she had little to gladden him. She told him it favored his father, hoping he would forget Brother Josephus and his sacrilege.

When he was eight, Christopher's grandmother died. What she thought was a touch of dropsy was in fact something else, and her belly swell up and she gone. Him grandmother dead when him eight but him stay on in de shack. De government men tek her body away fe bury dem say and leave him dere, never once asking if him have smaddy fe care fe him. Dem put she in a sack and pull de top tight. Before dem tek she, him tear she handkerchief in half like she once tell him fe do and put one half in him pocket and one half in her dead hand. To see her to her silent home and quiet the duppy's need for unrest.

"Me no want walk ya so till de end of time, mi son. Me no want fe roam wid chain 'pon me neck like rollin' calf."

After the men took her away, Christopher left the Dungle to find Brother Josephus. He had it in mind to beg the brother say a prayer over his grandmother. Him fine de cement-block structure, but inside the walls had been whitewashed and a woman working a treadle Singer in one corner tell him Brother Josephus gone to where him belong. No one said a prayer over his grandmother unless the government did such things.

He stayed on. The women and children in the compound did not want another responsibility and him was so sickly. Nuh mus' have TB. Him cough and cough. *Ka-hem, ka-hem.* Him back ben' so him lung dem never clear. But dem nuh tu'n him out. A where him fe go? Dem share wid him what dem fine, as long as de bwai him mine de other pickney and no cough 'pon dem.

When he wasn't minding the other children, he wandered the streets of the city, begging the tourists a few pence. But he was not at all a pretty child to them; he was ragged and dirty and dark and mauger, and he coughed before he could speak, and his brown eyes were already mapped with red lines, and his back was bent.

All that might have been forgiven, if when they spoke to him he came back at them with a Jamaican turn of phrase, something lilting, something in the mouth of a trickster, but he did not smile his eyes at the visitors; he hung his head, and they thought him stupid, or sullen. So he was not much of a success as a beggar.

He wandered into the Victoria Crafts Market one afternoon, but was given nothing, and was chased by a picture-postcard policeman who told him not to return. From there he found the docks along Harbour Street, where two big white cruise ships were tied. From the railings of one, high above his head, white people threw shillings and pence into the bottle-green scummed-over water. The shillings danced and flashed like Judas silver, while the pence dropped their dull copper selves heavily toward the sea. At the level of the sea the silver glittered briefly, lighting the surface, until the darkness of the water claimed it. The darker coins were lost fast against the harbor water, not catching the sun, sinking and hiding. Christopher watched as naked boys dove deep under the water, while people in soft shades, way above them, some flush-faced with excitement or reddened from the unfamiliar sun, grinned and shouted their delight.

Some boys emerged almost immediately, with coins grasped between their teeth or stuck into their cheeks, while others came up empty-mouthed. A few might not come up, but no one was keeping track. He walked back to the Dungle by himself. He could not swim. He had no skill at getting money.

Turning the pages of his grandmother's Bible he could not bring Jesus to life. He did not hear Him in his heart. The Word was beyond him. In his grandmother's iron bed at night he was frightened even as he fingered the power of her thunderstone. Fearing her duppy would flog him in the night. That he would have to turn her back with his left hand and she would cry, "Me two-time dead, oh!"

He would have lived and died in the Dungle and joined her in her wandering except one day Mas' Charles came to the shantytown to look for she. She came from the same countryplace as Mas' Charles; her sister was maid to his sister. He came to tell her that her sister had taken sick and died, and that his sister wanted her to take her sister's place. But the grandmother had been dead two years by then; her passing had not been noted in her homeland. Mas' Charles found Christopher instead and offered the ten-year-old boy the selfsame job. Christopher carefully folded the portrait of Lickle Jesus around the thunderstone and with these two possessions waited to leave his home.

Mas' Charles and him wife come by one morning to tek him to dere countryplace where de unmarried sister of Mas' Charles wait. In de cyar de woman complain dat him stink. She whisper hit to she husband but him catch de message. Him 'quash himself in de backseat, so him no tek up room and de smell of de Dungle be held tight in one corner. She tu'n 'round and ask him if him would open de window a lickle bit. She smile 'pon him. But she scare him. Him 'fraid fe ask dem to stop de cyar, so him peepee 'pon himself. She complain about de stink again an' about fe dem cyar seat— de man say no-t'ing. She tell de bwai dat if him gwan to do dat kind of t'ing him to sit 'pon de crocus sack him carry. Him tell she him will hold him water.

Dey move him into a lickle building next to de sister's house where him listen fe she voice, carry water, plant and harvest fe she, mend she fence, feed she cow and chicken dem, follow she to church. She keep him close.

In the air of the high-up country, with the riverwater and the fruit he could pick to eat, his cough eventually went away, his back straightened, and his life was spared. He was one lucky bwai. So de lady say. She came into his room one evening where he lay on his bed, an oil lamp lighting the visage of Lickle Jesus. She told him it was time for him to leave country and seek work in Kingston. He was grown, now, and she feared a grown man sleeping within ten yards of her house. She did not say this to him, just gave him a pair of long pants made of English tweed and fare to reach the city.

He took the bus across the island balancing his belongings in his lap. The hot tweed chafing his bare skin as he rode toward the Dungle. He sought news of his grandmother. He knew she did not rest. He felt her around him, loose. In the still starry nights in country, as spirits traveled the sky in light he felt her stir. Earthbound. Once he heard a whirring around him and his ears began to ring and in his panic and need for peace he threw the thunderstone into the darkness to strike the duppy he knew was there.

The thunderstone flung by God when his grandmother was a girl.

He would ask the women of the Dungle if dem know where de men tek she.

As the years in country stretched, his mind enhanced the Dungle. He was a bluefoot, a stranger, in the country. In the Dungle was his home, not in the room the woman put him, and then ask him to leave. He forgot his leavetaking from each place was equally silent.

When he arrived he found the settlement had been razed by the police—after the Conquering Lion of Judah visit in 1966—and the sufferahs were long gone. He found some resting against the ancient headstones in Maypen Cemetery, but they could tell him nothing further. He folded his crocus sack and went to sleep and found in the morning that someone had taken Lickle Jesus.

The same day he made his way up into the hills of Kingston to find Mas' Charles and his people dem and ask fe work. He had been a friend of the son, or so he thought, who stayed with his auntie on his school holiday. He and the son were playmates, as long as him finish him work first and don't get facey. In a few days he found these people. Mavis met him at the gate, after the commotion of the big yellow dog, and gave him casual work keeping up the grounds two days a week, told him he could not lodge with them, and advised him to walk through the hills over the city to find more work when they had finished with him.

He lived like this for several years, lodging with his women over the nights, or sleeping in the cemetery, eating from the patty shops, drinking at the rumshops, taking the bus or walking the hills to cut grass and trim shrubs and water flowers. He lived as he was used—hand to mouth.

People he worked for spoke to him only when they wanted something done, when they complained that he had not scythed the grass close enough, when they told him he drank his tin of tea too slowly. The bus conductors asked only for his fare. The shopkeepers only sought payment, for ten cigarettes, a glass of rum, a snack wrapped in paper. The men at the gate collecting for the sound system only wanted his ticket. The men at the political rallies he wandered into now and then told him where to fix his x and that they would change his life. And his women? Dem nuh jus' good fe spree? Big belly? Over the music at the sound system it was hard to hear their voices. If he spent the night with one of them in her lickle room behind the big house, they could not talk and took one another in silence, for the master and the mistress not to know him there. If the woman lodged with her mama or auntie in a yard in Trench Town, he had to listen as the mama or the auntie traced him as one hignorant bwai who 'fraid of duppy.

Like his labor, his connections to other people were casual. If he had thought about it, he would realize that there was not one single smaddy in the world who cared if he lived or died. His death would cause inconvenience to no one—unless him dead on dem property. In this loneliness he longed for his grandmother.

That Sunday morning he had not been hungry for food.

Before, he had stood in a rumshop in Papine, and as he got more and more black-up from the white rum, standing next to a man who said he was a retired policeman, Christopher saw his grandmother's face in the dark interior of the shop. He turned to the man beside him, who was talking as if he had some knowledge about the way things worked. He asked the man where he might find his grandmother's remains, speaking into the thick tumbler of clear liquid.

"Pardon?" the man responded.

44

Christopher told him he felt his grandmother did not rest; was possible to find she now and give she peace? He asked where the government put the bodies of poor people. Dem was all mashed together, or him could find she?

"How long she dead, bwai?"

"Thirteen Chrismus, sah."

Outside the rumshop some Jonkonnu dancers passed by with noise and drums, and with this festive interruption the man told Christopher he shouldn't dwell on death so. "Dis is Chrismus, man."

But Christopher persisted. "Wunna say wunna police, nuh mus' know dese t'ings?"

The man told him about public records downtown and that they would surely tell him what he wanted to know. If he signed some papers, the man said, then his grandmother would be released to him.

"Is true?"

"Yes, man."

Of course the retired policeman knew full well this was a hopeless case, but the bwai was so drunk and it was de Chrismus—nuh mus' give him hope? When de rum wear off, him nuh remember.

It was this hope that impelled Christopher to Stony Hill that early Sunday morning. As he walked across the city in darkness, he thought out exactly what he would ask Mas' Charles. His family, the people of his grandmother, work for the family of Mas' Charles long time now. Not too much to ask fe a lickle parcel fe him grandmother? Dis is de Chrismus. He convinced himself he wouldn't be refused. And yet he had nothing to base his conviction on—except it seemed fair to him—who had never experienced a piece of fairness in him life. But backra people could be soft around de Chrismus—dem who was so mean the rest of the time. Cyaan hurt fe ask.

Even with all this in his mind, with the ease given him by the rum, he was fearful. He walked down the hall, knocking the blade of his machete against the light-colored

45

walls, marring them. He hoped the noise would wake the master and the mistress, so that when he knocked on the door they would be relieved it was him and would be glad to see him. But the clank of his blade did not wake them, and he entered a darkened bedroom where the two people were fast asleep. He stood there, breathing down on them. So content. Happy in dem lot. Finally he shook the master's shoulder.

"What in Jesus' name!" Mas' Charles sat up in the bed. Content broken. Fright. A big brown man wrapped around in floral sheets. He pulled an arm free to reach for the pistol in the bedside table, but withdrew it when he heard Christopher's voice.

"Evenin', sah."

"Oh, it only you, Christopher." Relief in the brown man's voice. A relief which soon turned to anger, his heart pounding in his chest embarrassing him. "Bwai, what in hell you doin' here dis time of night?"

"Is one emergency, sah. Me have fe ask you favor."

"It cyaan wait till mornin'?" Harshness stayed in the man's voice. My God, there was a yardbwai in him bedroom. Askin' favor. Lord have mercy.

"Please, sah." Christopher was trembling. He looked down at his black rubber boots—his bare feet washed in sweat inside them.

"Look here, bwai. Dis not de time fe ask favor. Not a-tall, a-tall. Me nuh cya what kind of emergency. Nothing excuse dis invasion."

"Please, sah. Beg you 'ear me out. I talk to one man, police him say, dis evenin'." His voice rushed ahead in whispers. "Him say me can get me grandmother back. To give she funeral. Me know she nuh res'. She roam, sah. Me beg wunna one parcel 'pon you propity. Dat all. Fe bury she."

"Is when you grandmother dead, bwai?"

"Thirteen Chrismus, sah."

"You say, 'Thirteen Chrismus'?"

"Yes, sah. Thirteen Chrismus."

"Tell me again, bwai, for if me hear right, is true foolishness dis."

"She gone thirteen Chrismus."

"You hear dis bwai tell me him grandmother dead thirteen Chrismus? You hear dis?" The man addressed the shape of his wife next to him. Then he spoke at Christopher. "Bwai, you is one true jackass. Me nuh know when me ever hear such nonsense. Firs', she jus' dus' by now. Secon', no way in hell dem can fine she. Wunna damn lucky de man no try fe sell you burial plot."

How the man can ridicule him so? The fat brown man in the big fat bed wrapped in flowers grinned at him and shook his head at the ignorance of this stupid, stupid bwai. No wonder dis damn country don't amount to nothing.

"Sorry, massa. Sorry fe disturb wunna." He heard his voice made soft in apology. He fingered the piece of torn handkerchief in his pocket.

"You damn right, you sorry. You completely out of order . . . now get your damn self out of my house!" The fat brown man in the big fat bed looking forward to a morning of golf at Constant Spring while his wife was at mass rested his head back into his pillow. Christopher tightened his eyes. He asked his grandmother's forgiveness. "Be quick of hand, mi son. Be quick of hand." She spoke to him. He let go. A force passed through him. He had no past. He had no future. He was phosphorus. Light-bearing. He was light igniting the air around him. The source of all danger. He was the carrier of fire. He was the black light that rises from bone ash. The firelight passed through his feet and hands, and his blade quivered with his ignited fury. And him with the big fat mouth, his eyes shut against the conflagration of this tired drunken man, was astounded. He offered no resistance a-tall, a-tall. Taken by surprise in his contented half-sleep. Miss Evelyn murmured something into the thin morning air. "Lord Jesus. Lord Jesus." She began a rosary. That was all. They didn't ask to be spared. They didn't beg the fire-carrier to save them. The hard god. The lord of the

47

cutting edge. Christopher severed their ties to this life and left them to find their way into the next. Even now their duppies must be spinning through the room in confusion. No rest for them. No peace a-tall, a-tall. Dem would wander Stony Hill until dem drop. Turn to rolling calf spinning through the city. He left them in their confusion and wandered into the girl's room, where he released her soul as well. And when he finished there he went to find Mavis.

She saw the blood on his machete and the sweat which poured down his face, the blood spattered on his khaki, already turning to brown like the mark of sap from green banana and mango. Had she realized his lit passion she might not have spoken. "Lord have mercy, Christopher. Lord have mercy. What wunna done? Lord Jesus, have mercy on me. I see dem blood. Lord Jesus, de police gwan mek wunna hang. Evil, evil bwai."

" 'Ear me out. 'Ear me out. Dem provoke I. De man provoke I."

"Wunna no hab no business here dis time of night. Dem not gwan be angry wid wunna? What wunna expec'?"

"All me did ask was a lickle piece of lan'." He did not tell her the purpose of his request.

"What right wunna t'ink wunna have fe ask fe lan'?"

"Me people no wo'k fe dem long time? Dem no owe we sinting?"

He did not remember that in his request to the master this debt, this obligation of the master to him, had not been spoken. It was only to himself and Mavis that he spoke it.

"Wunna talk 'bout *owe,* bwai? Whatsoever wunna have, wunna owe to dem. Dem nuh rescue wunna?"

Lord Jesus, they were dead and she was still taking care of them. In death, as in life, their faithful servant. He swung the machete and she screamed, knowing there was not a living soul to hear her. He punished her in a terrible way, exacting not just silence but obliteration, and he could not have said why. He cut her like an animal, torturing her body in a way he had not tortured theirs.

After he had finished with her, he went into the kitchen and laid waste to their carefully arranged provisions. He smashed jars of food he had never tasted. And when he was through he made himself bacon and eggs, smashed the plate, and pissed on their wall. He emptied a bottle of Appleton Estate into himself, and with a sharp stroke against the wall made another weapon. He walked back into the bedrooms. The girl's room first, where he sliced her pinkish youth across. Then to the master bedroom. The master's penis was almost comical. Straight up from the crotch it stood until it met with the rum bottle and its jagged edge. Finally the mistress—left with a present wet with her daughter and her husband. He jammed it into her. He intended to end them absolutely.

He left through the front door, which he had never done, and found the dog roaming across the grounds, whining at the blood on Christopher's hands. He cut the dog's throat and left him under the white poinsettia he had pruned the week before. Then he went around the side of the house to wash their blood into the swimming pool, the chlorine bleaching his khaki free of stain. He rested on a chaise longue, waiting for the sun to rise and for their son to return home.

Paul emerged from the house. "Dammit, man. I forget it Sunday. De telegraph people dem not answering. We will jus' have fe drive to country and me will tell me auntie."

"Hokay, man."

As Paul turned, the machete made a wide arc behind him, blade cracking against vertebrae. Him nuh know what hit him, bredda; or did he?

It was ten years before. A light-skinned boy was calling outside the room of a dark-skinned boy. "Christopher, Christopher. It me. Mek we go catch some crayfish by de moonlight."

Christopher emptied Paul's pockets and returned to the site of the Dungle, where no one knew him.

"Whose baby was you, lickle Christ-bearer? Whose lickle baby was you?"

NO TELEPHONE TO HEAVEN. No miracles. None of them knew miracles. They must turn the damn thing upside down. Fight fire with fire. Burn. Yes, burn it down. Bu'n it dung, bredda. Catch a fire. Catch afire. Send flame through the hills like you light the cane. Watch de snake run 'way. No hab no choice in de matter. Do this or give up the ghost. Dem nuh kill Bob and tu'n him inna myth.

Cyaan tu'n back now. Capture the I in I. Then say Bless me Jah/Shàngó/Yemanjá/Jehovah/Oshun/Jesus/Nanny/Marcus/Oshun. I am about to kill one of your creatures. Some of your children.

3

THE DISSOLUTION OF MRS. WHITE

I have an assassin for a lover.
—Yoruban hymn to Shàngó

Boy Savage finally got his wish for a new life and embarked with his family for America—in 1960, when Clare, his elder daughter, was fourteen. Years later he would remark on the wisdom, nay foresight, of his decision—when he heard how Charles and his family had been chopped by some ungrateful gardenboy, a few among other sudden deaths.

The family flew from Montego Bay to Miami—fled, Kitty Savage said. In Miami, Boy found a used Plymouth for sale cheap on a flat dusty lot near their motel and bought it from a sympathetic *gusano,* himself newly arrived. Two island men, their islands visible across the water from each other on clear mornings, stood on the tail of a huge land-mass, speaking in their un-American tongues of the freshness of opportunity and the superiority of American automobiles.

The Savages loaded their possessions in the car that very afternoon and began their journey northward, New York

City their destination. Economy had dictated this method of escape, but Boy, as was his nature, spoke as if this were the perfect way to enter America, one which demonstrated his intelligence and bespoke their privilege. When in fact, the whole thing, the journey itself, came from a panic created by bad debts and racetrack losses, misfortunes, he told his wife, brought on by the boredom of being trapped on a small island and not the bad blood her family ascribed to him. He would put the immediate past behind him, he assured her. This was a new start in a new world. How could they not be thrilled by its prospect?

All became excitement, adventure for Boy—encountering but trying to evade the quiet apathy of Kitty, who didn't hold to metamorphosis and felt but homeless, breaking silence to tell her husband that he sounded like a character in a boy's annual. He ran on and on, spinning his head into the backseat to address his daughters—Clare and the younger Jennie. "Mind the road, man," came Kitty's sharp advice. But she did not quell him.

They knew about America mainly from the movies shown in Kingston; here, he told his girls, was a grand chance to find out about this country firsthand. The greatest country in the world, he stressed, since the Great Mother had turned socialist.

All traveling north in the bulky black car, that Kitty said "favor cockroach," were blessed to have such a chance at a new life.

No Statue of Liberty for them—oh, no—their emblem of welcome, going almost unnoticed until Kitty commented on it, was a small sign obscured by the cracked and boarded-up glass of an abandoned NAACP office they passed on their way out of Miami. A MAN WAS LYNCHED YESTERDAY, it said. "Hello, America," Kitty muttered to herself, after repeating the words on the sign for her family.

"Daddy, what is *lynched?*" The elder daughter spoke, not to her mother, but to the man whom she could count on to reassure her. The emotion in the car collided, and the girl knew the parents were at odds.

"It is a form of punishment for wickedness," her father told her—tidy and just, Dickensian almost. Like he had explained Tom Cringle's silk-cotton tree on the Old Spanish Town Road to her. Mus' be one old sign, he said to himself. Don't America finish with that business long time now?

Kitty sucked her teeth at his explanation but offered her daughter nothing more.

They stopped that first night at a motel in Georgia. Boy left his family in the Plymouth and went to the office to check in.

"Where you folks from?" the motelkeeper immediately asked Boy, after they had exchanged "evenings." His tone suggested challenge, rather than mere curiosity—concerned, no doubt, about the stranger's apricot color, which Boy would have explained as a suntan, given the chance—and the unfamiliar cadence of his voice.

"We are recently arrived from Jamaica," Boy responded, in his most formal, Jesuit-educated manner.

"Now, you wouldn't by any chance be colored folks, would you?" The man spoke at first with a patient hostility.

"I beg your pardon?" Boy stalled, and the innkeeper's patience vanished.

"Niggers!" He made a horrible harsh sound. "Because if you're niggers you can't stay here. You ain't welcome. It ain't legal." He paused to let the message sink into the alien's brain. "It don't matter where you come from. Mars. Venus. Timbuktu." The innkeeper smiled.

Boy, the bluefoot, barely touching the earth in this new world, wavered, quite struck by the man's directness. "Well," he responded, "we're not . . . ah, what you said." Glad that the black car with his slightly darker wife and mango and guava daughters was parked out of sight.

"Ain't that Jew-maica some little island off of Cuba?"

"Yes, that is correct," Boy immediately responded, not bothering to adjust the fool's pronunciation—better to let him think him get away with something—picking up the slur nonetheless.

"I thought only spics and niggers lived in those places."
The innkeeper, suspicion heightened because Boy had not
used *the word,* baited his prospective guest, not at all certain
who this man was. He cast his trained eye across the stranger's
face. Thin lips—but dark curly hair. Large nose—but no tinge
to the voice. Colored skin—but a manner that was quite
white. If this was a Negro, he had never encountered one
of his ilk before. Not so he knew it anyway. Still . . . it was
a tricky business. You could not relax for a moment. Someone might slide by. Sometimes it felt to him like the *Invasion of the Body Snatchers.* Who was real, who was not? Niggers were slick. Remember the county nurse with the bright
skin whose husband was the good old boy who ran the filling station and whose baby gave her away? The midwife
passed the story. The baby started brown. By the time the
news reached the center of town the baby was coal-black.
No matter. The man hightailed it out of town. The Board
of Health took the baby—silently. And the woman provided entertainment one bug-ridden summer evening during the Great Depression, when the innkeeper was a boy.
One of those nights it was too hot to do much of anything—
the least effort and you were bathed in sweat. But the people managed to rouse themselves and later gathered at the
river as the night cooled and enjoyed washtubs filled with
ice and Coca-Cola while the sheriff fiddled. Vigilance, his
papa said. Vigilance secured the safety of the people.

What shall I say to this man? Boy wondered. A lesson
from the third form on the history of Jamaica sprang to mind:
mulatto, offspring of African and white; sambo, offspring of
African and mulatto; quadroon, offspring of mulatto and
white; mestee, offspring of quadroon and white; meste-
feena, offspring of mestee and white. Am I remembering it
right? he asked himself. These Aristotelian categories taught
by a Jesuit determined they should know where they were—
and fortunate at that. In the Spanish colonies there were
128 categories to be memorized. The class of multicolored
boys rose and recited in unison.

The memory retreated as fast as it had come and Boy took the plunge, making himself at home in this new country. "I am a white man. My ancestors owned sugar plantations." There it was. Discreet but firm. No mention of personnel, but *slaves,* of course, jumped into the space between the two men, connecting them. An understanding was struck. As if this belly-burdened innkeeper could have sprung from the likes of Judge Savage, Boy's great-grandfather.

With this sudden clarification, Boy's manner changed from petitioning immigrant to ill-used scion. Pauper tu'n prince. No matter that at least one of the Jesuit's categories applied to him—no matter. He was streamlining himself for America. A new man.

"You wouldn't kid me, would you?" The innkeeper more relaxed but still distracted by the epidermis of the man before him.

"I wouldn't kid you." Boy smiled slightly. You stupid bastard, you make it easy.

"Well, then, welcome to Georgia and the Red Clay Motel."

"Thank you kindly, sir." Boy almost choked on the *sir,* well aware, despite his own presence of mind, that his wife could not be counted on and would tell the man soon enough who she was, should he ask her, should Boy allow him within range of her. He acknowledged the man's power over him. He said *sir.* To himself he called it "not sinking to his level."

The phone rang in the office. The innkeeper turned from Boy, spoke briefly into the receiver, and left to deliver a message to his wife, caught in the glow of the television out back.

Behind the counter across which the two men had spoken a collection of notices, postcards, signs clustered in a space of aged flowered wall. Guests were advised of checkout time, church services were announced, local attractions advertised. Boy passed the time during the innkeeper's absence scanning the wall, almost comfortable. Eyes moving from a framed dollar bill to the world's largest peanut to a five-legged dog in a glass case, on display behind a gas station on the northbound highway—on view for twenty-five cents. The face of a little girl smiled from a black-and-white photo beneath which someone had printed, in ink fading into the flowers, BUDDED ON EARTH TO BLOOM IN HEAVEN. Boy stopped there briefly, wondered about her, the absent man, then moved his eyes to a natural cross, pictured on a postcard, not to be missed, the legend said, a sign in granite of God's attention, laid bare by a farmer clearing ground. Somewhere a cockatoo on roller skates pulled a monkey in a chariot. RACIAL SELF-RESPECT IS NOT BIGOTRY, black ink on a white background promised, as if explaining the signpost beside it: YOU ARE IN KLAN COUNTRY.

Boy had seen *Gone With the Wind,* a very big hit in Jamaica, in an open-air theater near Lady Musgrave Road in 1941. As Atlanta burned, the screen turning that garish early technicolor orange, the skies of Kingston suddenly let go, and the spectators in the cheap unsheltered seats jumped the fences into the sheltered mezzanine, yelling all the while for Rhett and Scarlett to "run to rass before wunna bu'n up!" and for Miss Melly to "hole on, gal, hole on." As their moviegoing finery dripped across their freshly whitened, moviegoing shoes. The hot rain ran in sheets across the screen, creating a strange effect, as the fires of General Sherman raged, unquenched. The rain retreated during intermission and the audience settled down.

The Klan of course was featured in the movie—a chivalric organization, Boy was given to understand, filled with the likes of gentle Leslie Howard. The man who had challenged him favored Wallace Beery.

The innkeeper returned and Boy started, frightened the man knew what was in his mind, at least that he saw where his guest's eyes had stayed.

To further his acceptance, secure his family's safety, Boy questioned the innkeeper politely. "Are you a member of the Klan?" As if he were asking, "Are you Catholic?" "Did you go to Oxford?" He did not want to distress the man.

Once in, you could not let down. Even Boy had not believed the Leslie Howard–fraternal organization presenta-
tion of the white-sheeted disgruntled gentlemen scaring the
gape-mouthed manumitted slaves into obedience.

When the man only stared at him, Boy went on.

"I couldn't help noticing your sign. . . . I understand
it is an organization with deep historical roots."

"That's right. . . . Anyway, how'd you know about the
Klan?"

"Oh, we are quite civilized in Jamaica, you know." Not
immediately aware of the absurdity of that statement at all.

They left the motel early next morning, all waving as
they passed the innkeeper's office—Boy's suggestion, of
course, got to keep things smooth. He explained, as they
drove off into the foxfire of the dawn, that there would be
fewer stops from now on and everyone would have to take
care of her needs at the same time. He said they needed to
conserve money and make time.

He pushed the '52 Plymouth as rapidly as possible over
the southern roads, past the unpainted shacks in the center
of small fields, their one light an omen for Kitty, who grasped
their distant presence as a reminder of *home*, their unseen
inhabitants as familiar, and commented to Boy that she had
no idea there was so much poverty in America.

"You *know* they put roads beside the poorest places,
man. Rich people don't want confusion going on around their
houses," he answered her, knowing full well the woman was
no fool but needing to quiet her.

At night, when the girls were asleep on rollaway cots
and he held on to his wife in the lumpy motel bed, they
talked softly. "It will be different in New York," was his
constant refrain in answer to her talk about poverty, about
the mauger children at the roadside, about the rundown
outskirts of towns they navigated through, about the goddam signs advising people of their limits. Kitty was fixed on

these signs. She persisted. She knew damn well why Boy took secondary roads and could not seem to find a bathroom when one was needed, so that they used the countryside more often than not. Why they avoided restaurants and bought their food in general stores. Why he made all the arrangements at the motels and suggested they keep to their rooms. She told him she was no fool. Then he told her it was not so much different in Jamaica, you know. "But at least there is not so much *hate*," she whispered into the air in front of her face. "There are no signs in Jamaica."

"Don't be so sure, darlin'," he said quietly.

Silence between them then. *Home* was different—she would hold to that as long as she lasted. She who was cut from home.

They were shipmates, as surely as the slaves who crossed the Middle Passage together. Even as Boy's enthusiasm persisted and Kitty's quiet grew on the journey north, the two were not as opposite as might seem.

Stopping in the nation's capital, Boy pulled them through the memorials and monuments, educating his daughters along the way, while Kitty reminded him of Marian Anderson and what the *Gleaner* had reported. Yes, he replied, in earshot of his girls, but Abraham Lincoln was an honored American—standing beside the seated martyr, dwarfed in his presence.

This was a huge, a difficult country and each was outside of it.

Upon the New Jersey Turnpike. The burning excess of the refineries lighting their way. Boy almost bursting now as he envisioned New York City for the girls. They made their way across the Goethals Bridge to Staten Island, passing the truck farms, slag heaps, small houses, rundown docks, neat churches, brick schools—across to catch the ferry to Brooklyn. On the boat they could see the lights give shape to Manhattan. The spike on the Empire State a delicate wand. On the other side, among flatter buildings, they came to a stop, and Kitty went into an all-night drugstore in Bay Ridge to phone her relations in Queens and get directions.

Darker than the Savages—from Kitty's mother's side— the relatives, who made them welcome and offered to put them up until they could find an apartment, were employed on Long Island, in a large house a train ride away, as maid and chauffeur. Working for a man named Mr. Saxon and his grown children, they kept strange hours—Mr. Saxon was an important man, a banker, they explained—and saw their own home irregularly. This late night, when the Savages reached their destination, the relatives had just returned from work, and were dead tired, but stayed up nonetheless to offer food, brought fresh in shopping bags from Mr. Saxon's kitchen, ask news from home, and give their advice to the new ar- rivals.

Winston, a man of fifty, his hair sparse under the navy chauffeur's cap, came straight to the point. "Unnecessary struggle is for fools," he said.

Grace, his wife, wiped her hands on the pink nylon dress she wore, slightly stained from a day of picking up Mr. Sax- on's house. "Winston speak true. Pass if you can, man. This not a country for us. No bother with the aggravation . . . for dem love to give aggravation."

"What you mean?" Kitty asked her cousin.

"I mean," Grace continued, "the Americans dem don't understand Jamaicans dem. This not our country. Dem have dem own rules. The Black people here not from us. The white people here not from us. Maggie, the cook in Mr. Saxon kitchen, an American Knee-grow, so she call herself, give me as much contention as the man himself . . . and she cyaan pay we salary."

Kitty and Boy sat quietly and listened. The girls were asleep in another room.

Winston picked up the lesson where Grace left it. "Don't make any sense a-tall to make yourself miserable. Don't suf- fer fe dem sake. What dem don't know not gwan hurt you."

"But we nuh trap ourselves?" Kitty's voice alone.

61

"No, man." Winston came back at her. "You mek some dollar, you go back home. Is what we plan to do. Mek enough to pay down on a lickle house in Cherry Garden, then we gone like so." He clapped his hands together sharply.

"But what if we never get back?" Kitty questioned through the echoes of the handclap. Boy was silent.

"Nuh mus' get back? Is nuh home?" Grace put an end to the conversation as weariness descended on the company.

A few months later, in an apartment in Brooklyn, Boy picked up the telephone and it was Grace, asking to stop by on their day off to spend time and see how Boy and them was doing. Boy hemmed and hawed and Grace understood. She said she would make it another time but never called again, and the Savages were not asked back to Queens for evenings of rice and peas and curry chicken and fast games of dominoes and playing mento on electric guitars and marimbas and congas and claves. Children dancing and then dozing among unfamiliar clothing. Evenings when Grace and Winston saw some light in the time they gave Mr. Saxon and gathered other Jamaicans working similar jobs.

One connection had been broken. "Look like dem tek we advice, Grace."

"Look so, bredda."

Nothing of substance was spoken between the Savages and the cousins. Whoever received news from home would pass it on. But Boy began to call them Kitty's distant cousins, and she worried at their loss.

Boy had no visible problem with declaring himself white. It was a practical matter, he told his wife. There was no one to say different. And he said it in not so many words. He told people he was descended from plantation owners—and this was true. Partly. With each fiction his new self became more complete. His color fixed in those earlier centuries as if he had been birthed then. Robert Browning come to Brooklyn. Boy took up painting and decorated white china plates bought in bulk at seconds shops with the Savage family crest—mongoose and Moor rampant, *mihi solicitudo futuri*—arched at the center in gilt. He displayed his creations around their apartment, balancing them on the dark wooden ledge which ran a foot below the ceiling. Kitty made gentle game with his pastime but offered no resistance. It kept him home at least—and he needed it.

When he tired of china plates and there was little space left on the ledge, he moved to slabs of wallboard, painting his images of the great houses and the past. Louvered windows. Iron-railed verandahs. Bleached limestone. Some caught in high ruinate. Contained by vines and other growth. With black paint he taught himself to draw cracks across the façades, delicate spidery lines.

Kitty said her life was nobody's business. And then there was the day when she wandered through a graveyard in Brooklyn, near downtown, the cemetery of a large old Episcopal church, where she spied an ancient stone, cut hundreds of years before, marking the passage of Marcus, no other name, a man born in Jamaica, a slave to some family, who had been frozen to death crossing the water during the perilous winter of 1702. She passed her fingers over the letters cut into slate: F A I T H F U L S E R V A N T. And she feared she would join him.

She bent down and pulled a few wild violets from Marcus' grave and took them home and pressed them into her mother's Bible.

During the summer of 1960 the Savages watched Wilma Rudolph run in Rome at the Olympic Games, where she won gold medals wearing tennis shoes. Much was made of this. Tall, dark, lanky, with a willful grace, she made Kitty think of Dorothy, at first her girlhood companion, then her maid in Kingston. She remembered her, then she returned her to the back of her mind.

The Savages watched the Black runner on their rented nineteen-inch portable television set, hearing the Italians cheer on La Negra, as they named her.

The Savages lived in a small apartment in Brooklyn, in the basement of a three-family frame house, painted yellow with a black trim. Their '52 black Plymouth Cranbrook with fake black and yellow tartan seats was parked in the cracked cement driveway, the sparse city grass between the cracks tickling the underside of the car.

There were Italians above and around them, people who grew grape arbors in their backyards, put up thick red wine, and planted tomatoes by emptying the contents of Progresso and Contadina plum-tomato cans into well-defined and fertilized furrows. The tomatoes that grew from the cans were unlike any the Savages knew. Deep-red inside and out, they seemed to hold sunlight and had a sweetness that filled all three stories of the house when the women inside boiled them down to make their own tomato paste. Italian tomatoes—from the old country.

The yards were all well-kept, tidy and small, and the neighbors were generous in wanting to share their produce, but the Savages kept tightly to themselves, especially after one of the neighbors, a Mr. Antonelli, told Boy he understood only eggplants—he used the Italian word, then explained the metaphor, showing Boy the smooth purple skin of the fruit—came from the "islands." Poor Boy—people in America seemed always to be making that particular mistake, and always lumping the islands together, with an ignorant familiarity, as though they were indistinct places, sharing history and custom, white sands and blue waters indiscriminately. The man was a fool, like the innkeeper was a fool—but Boy let go of any outrage, if he felt any. He was not equal to this.

Kitty did not speak to the women around her; their accents clashed and they said they could not understand each other. She soon learned to travel out of the neighborhood and, forsaking the *salumerias* close by and the *bodegas* some blocks away, found a passage into Bedford-Stuyvesant, where in between the high-priced ghetto-specific chain stores she discovered shops from *home,* as if they had been airlifted intact, the only difference being that in Brooklyn the shops were not found in the shade of a stucco arcade, the goods held safe behind a stainless steel curtain in the night. These were small, crammed, glass-fronted shops, but they smelled so strongly of home that any other difference became superficial, in response to a changed climate, and not substantial.

Kitty mastered the route by subway and returned with mangoes, yams, cho-cho, saltfish, plantains, callaloo, goatmeat, and Jamaican curry to rub it with. She came home with these things laden in her arms, as if to say, Family, this is for you. In these shops she broke her silence, here she felt most the loss of home, of voice, even as she brushed the loose dirt off the yam-skin, imagining its origin in the bush, stroked the rough green lips where the cho-cho split, stuck her finger in the sap where the mango had been joined to the tree, remembering how it could burn and raise a sore. Resisting a desire to rub the sharp stickiness into her nostrils and around her mouth. In these places she was unto herself, speaking to the shopkeepers as if solitary.

Once, when the neighbors called down from a back window to complain about the smell of the curry, Kitty went out immediately and bought something called Air-Wick, a nasty-looking strip of wet green felt, anchored by wire, that emerged from a green bottle, reeking of a green chemical, with which the bottle was filled and which was supposed to remove all odors from the atmosphere. Instead, it seemed only to mask other smells, placing its own acridity over their sharpness or sweetness, distorting garlic, curry, tomatoes, and the smells of people. This was something new again. Like sticking a thick white plug into yourself, instead of letting the blood flow onto a folded cotton cloth washed in sweetwater and bleached in the sun. The green bottle with its foreign mission sat on the blond-veneer coffee table in front of the folding bed that served the Savages as a couch in the daytime and became Clare and Jennie's bed in the night. The table, like most of the furniture, had been bought at the local Salvation Army—but not the beds. Kitty said that beds had to be bought new, as you never knew who had slept in them before and what the mattress might be harboring. A used bed might have experienced the death of someone—of cancer, or TB, two of the scourges of Jamaica. Her point of reference—the place which explained the world to her—would always be her island.

The Italian women called across the clotheslines and yards and fences to each other, their conversations sounding a constant background, embroidering the events of their days and nights, difficulties, celebrations, marriages, recipes, scandals, brand names, patterns, and the news of the movie stars—their marriages and deaths. Why did they matter so?

The dogs were howling. Oh, God, they were howling like she had never heard dogs howl before. It was an early morning in April. What was making them howl so? The charge in the air—had it changed? Did they smell storm? Was there a shift in the wind? A quickening? A flat stop? The light—had that gone from darkness to the yellow-over-dark before a hurricane? But this was not hurricane time. A false dawn—was that their reason? God, she had never heard dogs howl so, and it frightened her. Had the palms bent over to brush the newly poured sidewalks in front of the house—waiting, welcoming the downpour? She listened for the *swish-brush* of the fronds glancing the concrete—she heard nothing but the almighty howling.

As she raised her head to look out the window past Boy's sleeping profile, the sky was becoming red with sunrise. Clear. No storm. No sign at all. They were in Kingston, living in a rented development house near Hope Gardens. A house, like the sidewalks, newly poured. All around them was unfinished. She could make out the shapes of dogs in the yard. Strays among those belonging to other families. Their heads raised, their mouths pinched into circles. Some with prominent rib cages. Some fatted. Some with tags glinting. Some with flaccid teats. All howling. Joined in something. In the slender bermuda grass, newly planted, already out of control, they stood. Gathered under the almond sapling.

Kitty was trying to rid the dread which had settled into her. She was terrified and did not know why. Trying to focus her mind on practical things, she thought she would have to cultivate the place around the trunk of the almond sapling, wash it down. The dogs most likely had peed against it. She would take her hand-fork that very morning and aerate the roots and put down some bone meal. She lay on her stomach and noticed that she had pulled all the sheets away from the bed. The mattress was naked except for where Boy slept, in a deep rum sleep.

The sun—a vivid disk—was up behind the one-room cement building Dorothy lived in. All of a sudden, Dorothy was at the bedroom door. Pushing it in. Frantic.

"Lord have mercy, Miss Kitty; why de dogs dem mek such a racket?"

"Me no say, Dorothy. I really don't know."

Dorothy had some idea, but according to custom tested her mistress first.

Earthquake? Kitty grasped at the one natural upheaval she'd not thought of before. No. Not so.

"Dem say dog only howl so when smaddy dead. Is one communication . . . it signify death. Wunna no recollect what dem tell we?"

"Oh, God," Kitty moaned into her mattress, remembering this truth of their girlhood. So it was. So it is. Raising her head, Kitty whispered to her maid, "Is what dem say, missis, is what dem say."

The dogs had not let up at all. Dorothy spoke again. "Den who it can be? Smaddy fe wunna, or smaddy fe me?"

"Lord Jesus, Dorothy!" Boy was finally awake. "Kitty, make her stop her goddammed yelling and leave us get our sleep."

Through it all Dorothy had not once raised her voice. She spoke desperately in whispers. The dogs had woken him, but he remained ignorant of this.

"Sorry, sah . . . is de dog dem, sah. Dem is inspired by death. Dem come fe tell we."

"You want us to tek you to asylum, girl?" The master threatened the woman.

Dorothy fixed her eyes away from the master's body and gazed into the yard. No threat of his could match what the dogs promised. She looked out and took her voice into a new cadence, a fuller volume. "Yea, dogs are all around me; a company of evildoers encircle me; they have pierced my hands and feet—I can count all my bones—they stare and gloat over me; they divide my garments among them, and for my raiment they cast lots. But Thou, O Lord, be not far off! O Thou my help, hasten to my aid! Deliver my soul from the sword, my life from the power of the dog!" She so stretched the last word that Kitty felt it vibrate against the iron bars of the window as the sound moved into the yard. Dorothy closed her eyes.

"Jesus! Jesus Christ!" Not supplication, but violent impatience in Boy's voice.

"Is nuh Jesus dat, sah. Is David, the King," Dorothy teased her master.

"Girl, you gone mad! You damn mad!"

The two women in the room caught each other's glance, as the dogs howled on, ignoring the man into silence. He could never understand these things as they did. The man was citified.

"Go put yourself in the shower, Boy." Kitty dismissed her husband. He left in silence—naked—and Dorothy remained. She had backed into a corner of the room, retreating there, turning her eyes from the master's body. What right him have to put him nakedness 'pon she?

"Can sit here, Dorothy"—Kitty patted the side of the bed—"as long as him in the shower."

Dorothy walked toward her mistress and cotched herself at the edge of the bed next to Kitty, ready to jump should the water stop in the next room. "Yes, missis."

"Dorothy, please take my hand." But Dorothy made no move, unused to such familiarity, instead lowering her eyes, considering the creases in her knuckles, drawing the skin tight across as she clenched her hands.

Tek she hand? What on earth was the woman thinking?

The woman in the bed, suddenly cold, was thinking from where her knowledge had come. She was thinking about the magic which had encircled their girlhood, which their stolid schoolmaster in the tiny country school had persisted in calling naïve science, bunga nonsense. He would mock her thoughts now, as he once mocked a girl who came to school with a crocheted bag of asafoetida pinned over her heart, saying she had seen Sasabonsam, and him out fe tek she spirit. He had warned them about false knowledge. That which was held in the minds and memories of old women. False prophets and false prophecies. Incantations. Blessings. Herbations. Libations. Number magic. Dirt magic. Water magic. Stone magic. Fire magic. Bush magic. The women intimate with the heavens and the movement of the heavenly bodies.

If it was false why it didn't disappear? Why did she respect it so? Why did the howling dogs bring her to deep terror?

The death of someone close to the hearer. As soon as Dorothy spoke it, Kitty remembered its promise.

All the psalms and gospels could not neutralize this knowledge—turn it to artifact, anthropological detail. The old women would say de Bible possess magic too. It all magic. The Bible only proved the ancient wisdom to be true. Her mother believed that. Her mother who kept church and read the Bible and considered the meanings embedded in one verse over the course of one week. Her mother intent on symbol. Her mother believed in other old women, just as she believed in the events of Gethsemane. Just as she believed in planting when the zodiac was favorable, and knew

69

which sign responded to which vegetable or fruit. Just as she arranged her flower garden according to plan. Just as she taught her children to fear Sasabonsam. To honor the Merry Maids in the river, for they brought eloquence to women. Just as she carved her calabashes with shapes she had been taught as a girl. Lightning bolts, a sign the spirits were alive in the heavens. Flying fish, the promise of resurrection. The eye of God. His merciful hand. His wrathful hand. His face moving across all creation. Four points of light—the moments of the sun—the solstices and equinoxes—telling the believer life might be without end. And the righteous return as a spring in the Blue Mountains. A rock in the river. A tree bearing Ethiopian apples. The sun-warmed swallowtail.

The woman in the bed was thinking about her mother. About her mother's coolness, holding, always holding, her knowledge, the things she understood, as the most precious to her, embracing these things more freely than she held her own children.

The worst possible loss she could dream of at this moment. To lose the one who taught me everything. Underneath was something else—something physical nagging at her. Kitty thought at that moment like a child. Lying on her back in that naked bed, the figure of Dorothy beside her. If I speak it, then it can't happen. Unless it has already happened.

"Dorothy, I don't know what I would do if Miss Mattie dead. What if it she?" She spoke to her maid exclusively, as if this would be her own loss entirely, not giving room at all to the fact that Dorothy had been one of Miss Mattie's adoptions, and that Kitty and Dorothy had wet the same bed when they were small.

"Nuh mus' go on." Dorothy rose in a sudden cool from the edge of the bed and walked out of the room. Out of the mistress's earshot she sucked her teeth. Dem never change.

When Boy and Kitty were finally dressed and drinking coffee, Boy having driven off the dogs with the full force of

70

the garden hose, telling Kitty she was stupid if she believed that nonsense; when they were sitting at the small mahogany table in the dining room, the telephone rang. It was Kitty's elder brother, Frederick, telling her what she already knew—Miss Mattie was dead. In her sleep—peaceful, peaceful, he kept saying, calling his sister Quit, her childhood nickname, which he had not used in twenty-five years. She had been a small child and ran everywhere, wanting to keep up with everyone, into everything, and so they named her after the bananaquit, with its quickness and fast-beating little heart.

The funeral would be the day after next, in St. Elizabeth. Boy seized on this immediately. Now there was no reason to stay in Jamaica. They could make new lives—they must make new lives. Kitty wearily agreed. And soon after she buried her mother's body they left for America.

She dreamed she was on a clay road heading into a gully which at first seemed quiet and then gathered sudden strength. A car washed past her. Then some animals. Roots of old trees were at once exposed and twisted by the force of the water. A cow dropped a calf as she became entangled in the once-hidden roots. The water washed over them, taking along the placenta and the caul which wrapped the calf. The mother washed from her perch, but the calf stuck fast. Boy shook her. The plane was circling Miami.

When she dressed her mother's body—being the only blood-daughter left on the island—when she dressed her mother's body, it was the first time she remembered seeing her mother's nakedness. This secret thing which had been hidden from her for thirty years became hers, for she was the only member of the family entrusted to it. The breasts full—the nipples dark—were stiff with lifelessness, and she caressed them. From somewhere came an image of a slave-woman pacing aisles of cane, breast slung over her shoulder to suckle the baby carried on her back.

She kissed her mother on her eyelids and rubbed coconut oil across her body, into the creases and folds, softening the marks of childbearing and old age.

Her mother could not respond to her. Where had she gone? Where were her ideas? Her beliefs? Where were her mind and memory? It seemed impossible that these things could have vanished into thin air. A black spider lighted on the back of Kitty's hand and made her ashamed.

She wiped off the coconut oil and bathed her mother with bay rum. The sharp astringent smell of alcohol cut with laurel mixed with the sweet heaviness of coconut. Kitty may have thought that these ointments and the tenderness with which she applied them might have made the difference. But the heat was fierce that afternoon and the smell of her mother was high.

She turned the mirrors to the wall. She swept the room, sweeping out the dead. Throwing the contents of basins into the darkness of the coffee piece—repeating, "We done wid she now. We done wid she now. We done wid she now."

Boy drove a truck for a laundry in Brooklyn and Kitty took a job in their office. She did clerical work, of which there was actually little, filing and typing mostly—she was the office girl. Catching water from the tap in the basin in the one washroom to make coffee in a stained percolator for the boss, fetching him doughnuts from the bakery two blocks away, dusting the confectioner's sugar from the desk where it settled like a pale pollen.

Because there was little clerical work, she was also assigned the task of sending out "helpful hints" to the laundry's customers, sticking them into the stiff plackets of the shirtfronts or between the folds of bedsheets in the back room, where the packers—two middle-aged Black women—bundled the cleansed linen for delivery. Kitty sat in the middle of a long aluminum table, between the two women, receiving the as-yet-untied parcels of cloth from one, slipping in her advice, except it wasn't *her* advice, not yet, then passing the parcel to the third woman at the table. All was accomplished in quiet.

The advice varied only superficially, always concluding with the reminder that customers continue to use the services of White's Sanitary Laundry, est. 1945.

Kitty signed these notes, an authentic touch, in the name of Mrs. White, the imaginary wife of an imaginary man, conceived by Mr. B., the proprietor of the laundry. Mr. B. had Mrs. White's messages printed by his nephew Louie, who operated the printshop a few doors away. "A good boy," Mr. B. called him, even though Louie must have been forty at the very least.

Mrs. White and her philosophy of laundry, and thus her philosophy of wifehood, of which laundry was but one office, was the creation of Mr. B. Describing in his quaint sweet language that it was a wife's duty to make her husband's shirts, their crispness and their stiffness, a matter of her primary concern. That it was part of her mission to assure "sanitary sheets to bless the slumber of your loved ones." That a woman might be held to account if her tablecloth showed tattletale gray.

The word *sanitary* was important, a keystone, to Mr. B., who remembered a not-too-distant time of rooms jammed with darkness, people, and little else. No light once you walked into the hall and shut the street door behind you. Nothing green except the pale cabbage simmering through the rooms. The only water from a rusted tap shared by ten families. Crowded together, whether in tenements, sweatshops, on the docks, or in the streets, where their voices raised to be heard and split the air. He could see the peddler clothed in scales on Friday afternoons, aging merman hawking halibut or cod, as the day wore on his stench stronger, the fish cheaper.

Mr. B.'s concern was White's Sanitary Laundry; across the street was the United Sanitary Meat Market, two blocks away the Excelsior Sanitary Bakery.

To accompany Mrs. White's words, Mr. B. fashioned an image which decorated each page on which her hints and reminders were printed. Such an American image. In carriage. Physiognomy. Presence. Wisdom. Good nature. Part altruism. Part salesmanship. Inspired by Fay Bainter, Selena Royle, Jane Darwell, as Mr. B. sat in the Brooklyn Loews during the Depression, perfecting his English.

An older woman with gentle gray curls, pink skin, two places on either cheek where the pink deepened slightly, soft rounded bosom, small mouth. Her lips indicating a smile that was not so much a reaction to something as a constant in her countenance—reassuring, never mocking or making fun. Her understanding nature accentuated by her tilted chin and clear blue eyes. Slender sculptured nose ending well above her smooth top lip, which had absolutely no hint whatsoever of the dark spiky hair that was common to all the older women in the neighborhood, who, after all, were not Americans and who had nothing in common with this image.

The jobs at the laundry were the jobs available to the Savages. An education in colonial schools, Jesuit or otherwise, did not seem to go very far here. And their previous experience—selling Scotch whisky and registering the names of tourists in a hotel log—seemed out of place.

They were ill-equipped. There was also the problem of their accents. Even if their credentials were of the highest, their skin of the palest, their accents unsettled most employers. Except Mr. B., whose own accent was very much with him. "It is not so much your accent, my dear," he once told Kitty. "It's that it is strange . . . I mean in the unfamiliar sense . . . to most Americans." He paused. "By now people are used to certain sounds . . . it confuses them when there are new ones . . . especially from exotic places . . . you know what I mean. . . ." He let his voice trail, shrugged, and sighed. He was, after all, a realist.

For the moment Boy and Kitty worked quietly, looking to further opportunity. Boy picking up white nylon bags filled with dirty clothes and linen, and delivering the carefully folded and tied parcels of laundry. Kitty using her voice only as Mrs. White, or as the office's quiet girl. Saving her twang,

74

her talk of home, for the shopkeepers of Bedford-Stuyvesant. Until Boy told her it was too dangerous, he felt, for her to travel there alone, or with one of their daughters, and he had no desire to accompany her.

He was making himself at home. Settling in. Branching out. Getting his information at the local bar where he stopped each evening, glancing at the ball games on the television suspended over the dark wood counter, telling his stories to the other workingmen who rested their behinds on patched plastic seats and drank Schaefer on tap. He didn't tell these men about his wife and her visits to Bed-Stuy. He listened as they talked on and on about the residents of the place—their displeasure turning ugly, so ugly that if Boy cared to defend the people his wife felt at home with, he would have been afraid to. He held his tongue, neither agreeing nor objecting. Silent in his mestee/sambo/octoroon/quadroon/creole skin. They naturally took his silence as acquiescence, believing, against their better judgment, that there was the son of a plantation owner in their midst—which is how he introduced himself.

Kitty did not cease her visits to her home away from home, but she limited them and did not talk about them, not telling Boy when she went, not taking the girls along with her, not bringing food from home, home to them.

She lived divided, straining to adjust to this place where she seemed to float, never to light, the shopkeepers of Bed-Stuy her only relief. She questioned why she was so miserable—and immediately responded that her mother was dead. Her mother would not have approved of her—her mother who told her to make the best of it. Whatever *it* might be. You lie wid dog, nuh mus' get up wid flea? Her mother's comment whenever Kitty quarreled with Boy. She smiled at the memory of it. She felt her mother's loss, keen. But there was more to her discontent, that she knew. She was not at home with pretense.

Time went on. After some weeks at the laundry, Boy got himself a position as a television repairman through someone he met at the bar. It was still laborer's work, but paid a good deal more than driving the laundry truck. His hope grew. Meanwhile, Kitty remained at the laundry, moving between Mr. B.'s office, the bakery, the washroom, the packing room, the want ads, the interviews. Day after day.

Soon it was late summer. One afternoon Kitty took herself to a big bank near Montague Street. It must have been her fiftieth interview, she thought, as she trudged through the hot streets, her cotton dress sticking to the back of her legs. In the bank, she was ushered upstairs to a large white man with a blond balding head, who leaned across his fat cherrywood desk to take her hand. "How do you do, Mrs. Savage."

"How do you do," Kitty responded.

As they spoke—about his name and title, the job of receptionist and how vital it was, the weather, New York in summer, the heaviness of the air and when it might lift— the man eyed her curiously, stressing again the duty of a receptionist to create a positive impression on the public. Then he spoke a direct question at her. "And where does that musical voice come from?"

From one lickle piece of gristle in me t'roat, she thought to answer. Instead, she dropped her voice and responded, "I am a Jamaican."

"I see . . . I see." Silence. Then, "My wife and I have not had the pleasure of visiting your beautiful island, but we have heard all about it from our maid . . . ah, perhaps you know her . . . her name is Winsome."

Of course. Kitty ceased listening to the man, letting his inquiry hang in the air, waiting for a chance to get out. He began speaking again. She was thinking about Winston and Grace. Their jobs. Their advice. Her chance at departure came quickly enough. The man had risen and was obviously indicating a finish to their conversation, only slightly discomfited by the stone-woman across from him.

"But," he spoke in an assuring voice, "there *is* a vacancy in our executive washroom. Perhaps your husband might be interested?" His manner eloquent, his smile gracious. See, we're not so bad after all.

She stood and walked out.

The whole business might have seemed a small thing. Should she have expected better? And she had kept her dignity. It was he whose stupidity was made plain. Then why did she feel in the wrong?

She left the big marble and granite building—hard as dem heart hard, she muttered—and walked over to the old Episcopal cemetery and sat on the grave of Marcus, F A I T H F U L S E R V A N T. She wept. Then caught herself. This t'ing a fact of life. Face it, gal. Your mama counsel you not to venture where you nuh welcome. She took the subway back to the laundry.

Kitty and the women in the packing room—named Georgia and Virginia—spoke only from necessity. But when Kitty was in the outer office, not sitting between them, she could hear them chatting softly, laughing. The word *girl*, affectionate, was repeated often. That afternoon, when she walked into the packing room where the women were sharing a sandwich and fell silent on her entry, Kitty wanted to smash what was between them, the three of them, and shout "Me not dem!", the other them. She wanted to tell the women what had prevailed, who she really was, but she could not and held back, afraid of what they might think of her, knowing their own travels through the city would make her seem only like a cry-cry baby. A house-slave inconvenienced by massa whim, while dem worked the cane.

Unable to speak to them, she took her place between them, her feelings lit by a dim fury, sticking Mrs. White's messages methodically, automatically, almost instinctively by now, into the shirts and between the sheets. Reliving over and over again what had happened at the bank. The cemetery with her touchstone of a grave. Why hadn't she said something to the man?—on the one hand. Why didn't these women speak to her?—on the other.

Why had she maintained silence, calling it dignity,

through all the other interviews in which her musical voice, her golden skin, had become the center of conversation and the reason for refusal? Coward!

Her head began to ache. She took her ballpoint and, hiding the paper with her curved fingers, like a schoolgirl being examined, embellished one of Mrs. White's epistles—one announcing a two-for-one sale, a businessman's special on shirts. She drew a balloon from the upturned mouth of the benign lady and printed within: EVER TRY CLEANSING YOUR MIND OF HATRED? THINK OF IT. When Georgia raised her head to watch Kitty as she wrote, for the pace at the table had slowed, Kitty caught her eyes and said softly that she was repairing a printing error. She quickly stuck the message into the shirt pocket, a blue button-down Arrow, not unlike the one worn by the man who had so distressed her.

Later, on the subway, she thought about what she had done and worried less about the possibility of being found out—a woman creating her own noise was rarely attended—than the fact that she had done such a thing. Was she turning into a crazy woman? Like the one with sores who chanted on the D train? Or one of the women at home who talked to lizards and duppies? Who thought they could slip from their skin at night and follow the Old Hige, their raw flesh aflame?

No. She was not crazy. There would be plenty of time for that. She smiled to herself. No. She was lonely. She was angry. Yes. That was all.

Automatic writing, they called it.

It probably would not happen again.

Settling this in her mind, more or less, she took some pleasure in what she had done. Hoping some businessman would find her message. That she might be a flower on the wall as he was struck by Mrs. White's reprimand. How silly.

Then she smiled at the idea of Boy cleaning a white-man's toilet.

As she shifted in the subway heat, her skirt stuck to

her, more than perspiration. She rose and glanced behind and saw that the stain had begun. She left at a station two stops before hers and was grateful for the dim light on the platform. At the top of the stairs in the bright late-summer evening was a shop run by a woman from Puerto Rico.

Kitty sought the folded cloth she had been taught to use as a girl. She entered the domain of another island woman. The woman, one thick black-and-white braid wrapped around her head, stood behind the cash register in the front of the shop. Behind her was a shelf of sanitary devices and birth protection. Douches, jellies, pads, plugs, foams. The woman had arranged the whole into a pyramid, above which was a sign: SERVILLETAS, TAMPONES, Y CONTROL DE LA NATALIDAD. In the middle of the pyramid, enveloped by the goods for sale, blessing their offices, was a statue of the Virgin, aureole of gold, robe of gold, face and hands of dark wood. A plaque at her feet identified her as La Morenita, La Virgen de Montserrat. The woman smiled at Kitty as she entered, greeting her with a nod of her head and a phrase in Spanish. Kitty smiled and nodded in turn and indicated with her eyes that she needed something from the pyramid. "I am sorry; I speak very little Spanish."

"It is okay. I live in America long time now. I know English."

"I am newly arrived. I am a Jamaican."

"*De Jamaica?*" The shopkeeper gave the name of the island the Spanish pronunciation.

"*Sí, de Jamaica.*"

"*Bueno.* What can I do for you?"

"I am having my . . . the curse . . . you know what I mean." Kitty's eyes turned down. The woman did not quite get her meaning. The *curse* was foreign to her.

"I bleed . . . *sangre.*" Kitty made herself whisper.

"*Ah, sí.* You need some pads? *Tampones?*" The woman turned to regard La Morenita and her display.

"I was wondering . . . in Jamaica we use cloth. Folded. We wash it each time by hand. Do you have such a thing?"

Around the shop were touches of the woman's homeland. Unguents, balms, candles in glass cylinders with saints and virgins fixed to them. Kitty envisioned a drawer with folded cloths.

"No. No such thing. La Morenita and I are in America long time now." The shopkeeper smiled. "These cloths are not convenient in New York. There is not the privacy for women to wash them, and the sun is too weak to bleach them."

"I see." Kitty felt very foolish, like a homesick child. "Well, may I have a box of Kotex, please, *por favor?*"

"*Sí.* Of course." The woman removed a box from the side of the pyramid, then walked to the back of the shop, leaving Kitty at the register and returning a few seconds later with a paper towel wet with water and salt. She murmured *pardon,* and began to carefully stroke the back of Kitty's skirt. Kitty was at first embarrassed, then gave in to the woman's care.

The shopkeeper returned to her place behind the register and, as she rang up the sale, Kitty's eyes glanced over at the darkness of the Virgin. "What means La Morenita?"

"It means the little dark one. They say she was cut from the life. From ebony."

There was absolutely no visible outcome from Kitty's impetuousness. Probably no one paid any mind to Mrs. White. Powerless icon masked as mother. Kitty trudged on.

When it seemed, after similar interviews, similar insults, similar assumptions that because she spoke in accented language she was illiterate—when it seemed, after months in this new country, that she would labor forever as Mrs. White, walking the streets of Brooklyn on her lunch hours, visiting her home away from home in secret, traveling each evening back to the small apartment where she cooked dinner for the girls, waiting for Boy to reappear, now he had traded his paints for the camaraderie he found in the bar. She, watching the infernal television, thinking it would take her mind off her troubles, suffering as she was from a weariness which did not promise to leave her, wishing her life away, as the days got shorter, giving in more and more to Boy's warnings about Bed-Stuy, unable to return with the food she cherished—when all this got to her so she could not bear this place and the prospect of the cold with her thin blood, Kitty amused herself by sending more messages. They could hurt no one. No doubt she had been right and no one attended to Mrs. White or her silly hints—they would all end their journey on a garbage barge.

Her pen traced balloons and filled them in, putting words in Mrs. White's pert mouth.

WE CAN CLEAN YOUR CLOTHES BUT NOT YOUR HEART.
AMERICA IS CRUEL. CONSIDER KINDNESS FOR A CHANGE.
WHITE PEOPLE CAN BE BLACK-HEARTED.
THE LIFE YOU LIVE WILL BE VISITED ON YOUR CHILDREN.
MARCUS GARVEY WAS RIGHT.

Things did not really become difficult for Kitty until Boy found a sheaf of these pronouncements in her handbag while rummaging one night for cigarettes, and confronted her with them, waving them in her face.

"Kitty, for God's sake . . . what is this?"

"What you doing in my bag, man?" She was suddenly embarrassed.

"Never mind that. . . . What in hell are these?"

"In hell fe true. None of your business."

"Don't shut up on me, woman. You gone crazy? You want to lose your job?"

"Nuh gwan lose me job, bredda."

"You will if Mr. B. him find these."

"How him gwan find them? Chuh, man, is jus' something I do for entertainment."

Then quiet.

She was sitting on a second-hand straight-backed rocker staring at the television. Robert Young kissed Jane Wyatt on his return home and Kitty sucked her teeth.

"Busha, is maybe time we cut the cotta . . . what you think?" She broke the silence, addressing him as overseer, with reference to divorce among the slaves who had been among their ancestors. Slicing the device on which their burdens balanced. She spoke in code because the girls were in the kitchen washing the dishes. Still, her words fit.

"Why you call me 'busha,' woman? I don't drive you. I don't push you against your will." Boy, frightened.

She smiled at him. "You preffer 'slave' . . . 'massa'? Is what your American friends call you?"

Suddenly, she was in control. Silence again. And then he moved to kiss her and tell her he needed her and loved her more than life itself, and, as God is my witness, we will return soon. Soon as we get enough money. He put his arms around her and begged her just to be careful and not let Mr. B. catch she. That night they made love and he thought the cutting of the cotta was forgotten, not realizing, as she drew herself away to fold into sleep, she was not at rest.

She slid into a sleep in which she dreamed. On a green hillside she took to be her mother's land, ruinate, a small dark figure robed in gold and lit around by gold light was leading a procession. It seemed in the dream that La Morenita floated up the hill, as those behind her, unlit beings, scrambled and fell, tripping in the thick growth. Kitty felt herself present but did not see herself in the crowd. Darkness then. The light was gone. The dark lasted into confusion. Suddenly La Morenita beckoned through the dark, raising her arm, tongues of fire shooting from her armpit. They were inside the house of Kitty's mother, grown large in the dream. The fiery Virgin and the other pilgrims were gone. Kitty was left to find her mother in this house, which loomed larger than it had ever been. All was emptiness. On one wall was etched *This Do in Remembrance of Me.*

Kitty woke, prepared breakfast, dressed, and left for

work. It was time to end her nonsense once and for all. Once and for all. She took a stack of letterheads and colored in the pink face of Mrs. White. She drew a balloon next to each dark face. HELLO. MRS. WHITE IS DEAD. MY NAME IS MRS. BLACK. I KILLED HER.

She felt free, released. She spent the afternoon tucking the sheets of paper into clean linen. Sending her furious Aunt Jemima into the world.

She left at the end of the day and thought no more about what she had done.

When she returned to work the next morning, she was met by Mr. B., who was fussing around the office, scattering confectioner's sugar wildly in his passion. At first unable to speak to her, he pointed into the packing room. Kitty peered inside; the room was empty.

"Where are Georgia and Virginia?"

With this question the man caught his breath. "I . . . I . . . had to let them go."

"But why? They are good workers."

"Yes, and they have worked here for quite a few years and I have been very good to them. But look at this, my dear. Just look at this."

He thrust in her face a picture of Mrs. Black.

"Where did you get that?"

"Someone brought it here this morning. In person, mind you. As shocked as I was. He also brought instructions to discontinue serving as their laundry. One of my oldest clients . . . and there have been similar messages . . . telephone calls. . . . How could they do this to me? What did I ever do to them, except treat them right? I mean, it's not easy for them to find this kind of job . . . and they will starve before they get any references from me." He dusted confectioner's sugar from his vest. "But, you know, that kind is just no good. Unstable. You know what I mean."

Kitty barely shook her head. He explained.

"Something missing . . . something missing upstairs . . . a screw loose." He pointed to his head.

83

"I don't understand." Kitty was unprepared for this. "I just don't understand. Why did you fire both of them?"

"Because neither of them would admit to this . . . this desecration. But they always stick together."

"Mr. B., I did it. I am the one responsible."

"A nice girl like you? Don't be crazy."

"But I did."

"No. No, I can't believe that."

She took her leave that afternoon. Throwing the blasted letterheads into the wastepaper basket. She had committed an act of luxury. She had no way to reach either woman. And did not know what she would do had she that knowledge. That night she announced to Boy that she had had enough. In a week she took the younger girl, the one who favored her, back home, and told the elder one to look after herself and her father.

4

WHITE
CHOCOLATE

Où allez-vous ma femme marron ma restituée ma cimarronne il vit à pierre fendre et la limaille et la grenaille tremblent leur don de sabotage dans les eaux et les saisons. . . .

(Where are you going my maroon woman my restored one my cimarron it is so alive the stones are freezing and the filings and the pellets tremble their gift of sabotage in the waters and the seasons. . . .)

—AIMÉ CÉSAIRE, "Autre Saison"

Captive people have a need for song.

The thirty-six-year-old woman Clare Savage is standing in the back of a truck climbing through the Cockpit Country. Her story is a long story. How she came to be here. For she had once witnessed for Babylon. Had been ignorant of the wildness of the Maroons. There are many bits and pieces to her, for she is composed of fragments. In this journey, she hopes, is her restoration. She has traveled far. Courted escape. Stopped and started. Some of the details of her travels may pass through her mind as she stands in the back of this truck—NO TELEPHONE TO HEAVEN. She may interrupt her memory to concentrate on the instant, on the immediate and terrible need.

You have seen her before this. She was the light-skinned girl vomiting into the swimming pool at Buster Said's Christmas party. In her twenties then—visitor to her home-land. Not answerable to her place of birth. Citizen of another, greater, country. Student of the motherland. Motherless. Paul H. was someone she knew, not well. They danced the meringué the evening of the party and spoke very briefly—about how they might be related, money, England, Jamaica, America. "Hey, Jude." It was a stiff exchange. Their hearts were not really in it. Far easier for them to go into the poolhouse and wander over each other's bodies without speaking than to carry on a conversation. He thought her kind of cool, in the sense of standoffish, even after she let him stick his cock into her and moaned as he sucked her nipples. Even so, she seemed to want to get it over—he could tell—and moved away too quickly once he came into her. He was finished with her but used to girls drawing little pictures on his chest with their long nails afterwards. Something they imitated from the romance comics passed from hand to hand in the strict all-girls' schools. She said nothing, traced no little houses or palm trees across him, just got up and walked out of the poolhouse and back to the party. She poured herself champagne, filling one of Buster's mother's Waterford water tumblers to the brim, sitting by the pool alone. Until she threw up into it, and Harry/Harriet came over to her with a towel, saying, "Cock-juice don't mix with champagne, sweetheart," making her smile.

Paul was ignorant of this exchange, remaining for a while on his back on the air mattress, thinking this girl considered herself better than him. Nuh mus'? She had escaped the island, nothing held her here. Was living, going to university, in London. While he was stuck in his father's business and in his mother's house. Held fast. Chuh, man. Well, the girl could have London. It was cold and damp and filled with people who hated them. So dem say.

Clare could entrust her body to this boy she barely knew and watch herself as he fondled her and feel pleasure in her parts but still be apart from him. Feeling free, the word she put to it then. So apart, so free, she could walk away and be glad they were done with each other. Him with his postures, talk of his cyar, house in the hills, bird-shooting. As he spoke she focused her mind on her escape from this mess of a place in a few days' time. He assumed, like so many of them, that Jamaica was the world; he said so. Not realizing, or willing to admit, that it was only one of the saddest pieces of the world. But geopolitics was of course not the only thing that came between them.

When she heard the next afternoon, lying on the black sand at Cable Hut alongside Harry/Harriet in his/her Pucci bikini, his/her furry chest getting the odd stare, when she heard what had happened to Paul and his people, she felt shock but no real sorrow. She did not think of his sperm congregating in her, so that his line might not have ended. In a few days she bled. She was free of him. Free as a free-martin.

She watched people on the beach, listened as they stirred to the news, some with rum-stunned brains, in bright swim-suits against volcanic refuse and flawless sky, seeming only slightly more impressed than they had a week before, when news reached the beach of a man eaten by sharks after his cabin cruiser foundered in high seas and his right foot caught in some neger's fishing net.

They lived with the unexpected here. The sea.

A few tourists were scattered across the beach, ghostly, ignored—native color could be found here, someone tipped them—but they did not note any stir among the inhabitants. Were they expecting limbo? Their attention was soon drawn by a pink flounder of a woman surprised by a sinkhole. One of their own. They gathered the sputtering woman in their arms and returned to Courtleigh Manor, whence they had come. This place was too wild.

Jamaicans smiled.

Clare watched. Of these people.

These people who called the murders of the night before the *latest incident.* These people who made her think of her family. Not her father and mother—her mother was dead by that time, of a natural death. Her father was living in Brooklyn with an Italian-American wife. Her sister was a junkie in Bed-Stuy—shipped to the mainland a few years before on their mother's death. Slipping in and out of an American high school, she slid into the street.

Clare thought not of these disintegrated people behind her, former members of a shattered little entity. She thought of her mother's side, staunch to the island then, big fish in a little pond, her father would have said. Was their world about to come to an end? The pond scum vaporized by blue vitriol, cleansing the waters once and for all. No. Not according to them. No matter how many times a similar act happened—to those they saw at garden parties with cut-glass bowls of planter's punch displayed on white linen, those in the crescent drives of private schools to collect their uniformed children, those strolling their tidy well-dressed selves through the paddock at Caymanas, those eating salads at the Sheraton alongside aluminum executives, those congregating in the hills behind their stucco walls—no matter how many times it happened, and the happy few lost another member, they explained it away as an isolated incident, a single display of wuthlessness, of rude bwaihood, no more.

Clare turned the news of Paul H. and his family around in her mind, returned to the motherland and graduate school, and tried to forget the details for a very long time. Except they would strike her in flashes. Like when the Queen Mother, chancellor of her university, visited the Institute and Clare was chosen to greet her in the reading room. Along with other students, carefully chosen as to demeanor and looks—and the fact that they represented parts of the Empire. As she took the tiny woman's gloved hand, lowering herself into a curtsy, she thought to say, Did you know the boy I let fuck me over Christmas had his head cut from his shoulders? Small talk. For whom did she feel more contempt? The old lady standing in front of her, smiling like a parakeet, or the people, her people, who believed in isolated incidents and random violence and the sanctity of the birdlike old lady?

She buried herself in books.

90

*

You knew her also as the girl left behind in the Brooklyn apartment. The albino gorilla moving through the underbrush. Hiding from the poachers who would claim her and crush her in a packing crate against the darker ones offended by her pelt. Make ashtrays of her hands, and a trophy of her head. She cowers in the bush fearing capture. Waiting for someone to come. Crouching. Not speaking for years. Not feeling much of anything, except a vague dread that she belongs nowhere. She fills her time. In schools, playgrounds, other people's beds. In pursuit of knowledge, grubs, and, she thinks, life. Her loss remains hidden—over time a fine thick moss covers her skin. She does not speak of it. She does not speak of it. She does not gather branches to braid into a nest. She moves. Emigrated, lone travel, the zoologist would have recorded. Time passes. The longing for tribe surfaces—unmistakable. To create if not to find. She cannot shake it off. She remembers the jungle. The contours of wildness. The skills are deep within her. Buried so long, she fears they may have atrophied. Distant treks with her dark-pelted mother. With a solid urgency they may emerge but she must also give herself to the struggle. She belongs in these hills. And she knows this choice is irrevocable and she will never be the same.

She is the woman who has reclaimed her grandmother's land.

She is white. Black. Female. Lover. Beloved. Daughter. Traveler. Friend. Scholar. Terrorist. Farmer.

She is not cool in the standoffish way. Not now. She has a coolness that she nurtures. How she became cool is her story.

On the truck in the heat a question passes through her mind—we may as well begin here. A fragment of memory. "And why do you want a child from us?" The inquiry recalls a scene a few years before. In a yellowed nineteenth-century edifice, close, cast back, the inquisitor's voice clipped,

91

British, as if she is asking, "And when did you last see your father?"

Memory crosses memory crosses memory. She sees the dour Roundhead questioning the blue-suited Cavalier child in a painting she once scanned in a seminar on the reconstruction of the past in art. For the life of her she cannot remember the artist. Names fly in her brain—Holman Hunt, Burne-Jones, Watts, Millais—no, none of these. No. Give it up. But I knew once. Yes. Peering at the boy in her mind who is standing on a stool, as the mother and sister quiver in the background, terrified the son will be innocent, honest. Where does your father hide? Why have your mother and sister abandoned you to the inquisitor? She sees the painting full-color in her mind—all Victorian earnestness and literal-mindedness, she knows this aspect of the motherland—as she passes through the mountains of the Maroons, as far from the motherland as the mountains of the Moon, and the truck jolts. The painting dims and memory switches, once the truck has calmed and her hands relax from grasping the splintery sides. She remembers the apartment in Brooklyn, long nights when she waited dinner and her father did not return. His heaviness when he did. She was his dandified child for a while—until she left, suddenly. She recalls the original question which brought these memories. "And why do you want a child from us?" Her mind returns to the nineteenth-century edifice in Constant Spring. The voice of the inquisitor bounced in a building named for Lady Mary Wortley Montagu. Colonial contrivance. Institution for light-skinned foundlings. As was she. I expect I want a child from you because I want to save one from you, she thinks. Sharp, very fresh, my girl, but not completely true. Does she think a child will complete her? Make her whole? I want one with curly brown hair and green eyes. One who has no family to speak of. These are the facts as I believe them. But as you are no doubt well aware, there are no facts in Jamaica. Not one single fact. Nothing to join us to the real. Facts move around you. Magic moves through you. This we have been taught. This fact that there are no facts. Wait. I

92

can call up one fact. "The adamantine refusal of the slave-women to reproduce"—a historian report that. What of Gamesome, Lusty Ann, Counsellor's Cuba, Strumpet called Skulker—not racehorses, mi dear, women: barren. Four furious cool-dark sistren. Is nuh fact dat? Fact, yes, but magic mek it so.

In the end they wouldn't give a child to her. She was not qualified, they said. Had she a child would she be on this truck? On her way to restoration?

BEWARE OF THE 21 FAMILIES reads the graffito white-washed on a rock the truck passes. Her mind returns to the present.

After her mother left her, in the days before she started school, Clare remained in the apartment until her father reappeared, abiding by his rule that she was to leave the house on no condition. So she stayed in, keeping house and watching television, moving within the space of her loss. But not allowed to be lost because her father said the family would be reattached. Soon.

She was taken by the magic of the television, and of her ability to conjure images by a switch, to change the images as she wished. Jamaica had not this sort of magic, this curious and wondrous choice; all man-made images were channeled into the cinemas, whose programs changed once a week, and over these selections there was no control. The island took what it was sent, not so different from the little black box catching waves in the Brooklyn apartment.

Jamaicans came in droves to see the pictures, to glimpse the world beyond the island, lose themselves, whether in theaters or in country gathering places—the picturegoers carried the images away with them, transforming them, eager always for more. In the streets and in the yards, Brer Anansi, about whom their grandparents taught them, Rhyging, about whom their mothers warned them, Sasabonsam, whose familiar image terrorized them, mixed in their games with Wyatt Earp, Legs Diamond, Tarzan the Apeman, and King Kong.

Playing in the dusk with Alexander, the boy of four-teen who kept the outside clean, while Clare waited for Dorothy to fix her supper, evenings when her parents were away, each child became a movie character. Alexander being Paul Newman being Billy the Kid, asking Clare to be the girl he rescued. These were forbidden games. And when her parents returned early one evening and caught the two circling a wagon train, Alexander was fired and Clare was condemned by her father for being "as thick as two thieves with a gardenboy."

In the dark of the basement apartment, trying to dismiss her mother, she watched pictures. Pictures she had not seen before. A white-haired butler teaching a little white girl to dance down stairs. When her father came home, Clare mentioned the movie to him and he told her about Bill Robinson and how he had tap-danced up Broadway once. His mother had written him about it from America when he was a boy and she worked the stage. Boy explained to his daughter what Broadway was and the difficulty of Robinson's task. Tapping up the sinking-rising cobblestones downtown, up the pitted avenue into Harlem. He talked on and on, telling his daughter how brave Robinson was, not just in dancing up Broadway but in making his way through America.

When she asked about the little girl in the picture, her father said that she was Shirley Temple, America's favorite child—no more, no less. Nothing was said about the little girl being as thick as two thieves with a butler. This was another country. This was make-believe.

"But, Clare, you mustn't spend all your time in front of that thing, you know; for it is a true time-waster. Read a book. You need to prepare yourself for school."

But Clare did not stop.

A large Black woman cooking and singing and laughing for Claudette Colbert and Monty Woolley in *Since You Went Away*. Clare recognized the woman (the large Black woman wearing a tiny little white cap) from *Gone With the Wind* (white cap replaced there by a plaid tiehead), which the third form of St. Catherine's had seen at the Carib—during one of the annual showings of the film on the island. They were escorted by a teacher, a red-haired sunburned American woman who seemed confused. Who was led from King's Parade one Saturday morning for picking up a pair of pink pussboots in Bata's and neglecting to pay for them. Poor woman. Her color rose higher. Downtown Kingston is a very small place, where nervous red-haired white women stand out, and her story made the front page of the Sunday *Gleaner*. It was too good to miss. She assured the police that one of the other patrons had asked her to hold the shoes for a minute, and when the police didn't believe her, she told them she had fully intended to pay for them but had taken the shoes outside to see how they looked in the sun. She was, after all, a member of the faculty of St. Catherine's School for Girls, so she could be no thief. "Anyone can teef, missis," the constable told her.

"Nigger," she muttered—no one caught it.

Fired from school for causing embarrassment. Also for teaching the girls American history—she had told the headmistress she was a Canadian and would instruct the girls on the Commonwealth. A white woman washed up in Jamaica. What had possessed her to take on the American Civil War? Desperate. To lead, literally by the hand, a line of girls in burgundy tunics and sea island cotton blouses into the darkness of the Carib one afternoon when they should have been playing rounders, to see a "documentary," as she put it, of this "tragic phase," as she put it, of American history? Poor Miss America (which the girls called her behind her back; her name was Miss Peterkin), pacing the rows in the quiet cinema, telling girls impatient for the picture to begin, girls rustling their sweetie wrappers and surreptitiously slipping mangoes from their bookbags—exhorting them, in fact— telling them they needed to learn the lesson of the film, as the situation depicted therein was so similar to the situation on their island. Poor woman—where was her judgment? "Order is meant to be maintained," she stated vaguely to the fidgeting girls, whose color ranged from dark to light and back again. "A conflagration could take your nation down." Pause. "Do you want to forage for carrots and wear a dress made of draperies?" The girls kept silence, fighting the laughter in them. Her voice, already nasal in pitch, ran up the scale, out of control as her passion increased.

The picture began. Watching the burning of Atlanta, the teacher screeched suddenly, like a chicken disturbed at her roost, then bowed her head in tears. The girls assumed she was a fool.

She was the first American Clare ever met.

Sitting in the damp of the basement during a weekday afternoon, recognizing Hattie McDaniel, Clare remembered that other afternoon. She remembered the teacher. This led her to the other girls, her classmates, to whom she was not allowed to say goodbye because Boy owed the school money and was afraid of the complications should they find out Clare was leaving. So she didn't say goodbye. She merely disappeared from their lives. And they from hers.

Just like Miss America.

Once her mother and sister departed. Once the door slams in her head signaling their sudden return ceased. Once she realized the departure was not a mistake and was irrevocable. Once she lost faith in the *soon* she had been promised—Clare tried to settle in to life with her father.

The absence of the two other people was noted differently by each. Clare tried to wipe them from her mind, yet caught herself, even while watching the mind-wiping moving pictures on the television, passing her eyes and hands across still pictures of the family unit which she held in her lap. At these times she came to with almost a shudder. What had happened? Why was her mother gone?

Boy spoke often of his absent wife, speaking again and again his belief that her return was imminent. "Your mother will be back. Mark my words. Your mother will be back. Mark my words. Wait and see. She can't live without me."

Kitty wrote letters addressed to the two of them, which annoyed Boy. There was no question that she and her husband should cut the cotta, she wrote. Why should they? When Boy came to his senses he would return to Jamaica and the family would be one again. Meanwhile, Kitty advised, Clare should take her mother's place—it would be good training for her, she added, without conviction.

For Kitty and her other daughter, Jennie, there were two rooms at an auntie's in Mountainview Gardens. Kitty got her old job back. She was prepared to wait out her husband's stubbornness. *Absence makes the heart grow fonder*, she ended one letter. Could so easily turn to *Out of sight, out of mind*.

No one made a move. September came. Each partner seemed reconciled to the distance between them, talking of missing all the while. Boy took his daughter to the local school for enrollment.

The truck lurches. She grabs the hand of the comrade at her left. The matériel under the tarp shifts and rolls. Still the truck climbs. The sun has come out—hot. And the khaki is stuck to her back, and trickles of moisture collect under her breasts. When the truck steadies she lifts her breasts and blots the wet spaces with the khaki.

Boy took Clare to a high school. The principal, brass ornament indicating she was Mrs. Taylor, a woman with a flushed face and thin body, timepiece dangling on a chain around her neck, greeted the two of them, asked them to be seated. They faced her in heavy oak chairs. Immediately she told them it was a matter of course in New York City schools to have foreign students begin a year behind so they wouldn't get "lost." The woman stated this custom perfunctorily, expecting to quell any objection. Boy let her have her say and then suggested an exception might be made for his daughter—after all, she was proficient in Latin and French, was beginning Greek, and had studied algebra and geometry since she was ten. In addition the girl had read many of the classics: Dickens, Shakespeare, Milton. He rested his case.

The woman said this made no difference. None. "That

is all beside the point, Mr. . . . ah, Mr."—she glanced at the card in front of her—"Savage."

"I don't understand."

"We are professional educators here. We are talking about degrees of emotional development. Children develop differently. Children from underdeveloped countries develop at a different rate than American children. Believe me, it's for the girl's own good." She lifted the timepiece from between her breasts, glanced at it, allowing her abstraction to sink in. "I am sorry, Mr. Savage. I am sorry but that is our rule. There are no exceptions."

"I see." Boy acquiesced, never once asking where this was written, and could he see the guidelines of the Board of Education.

"Now . . . now that we have an understanding, let me go over the form with you. I will take down the information, to save you any difficulty with our language." She smiled at the man who spoke to her in the King's tongue.

Boy said nothing at all.

"I will take down the information and send it to the elementary school in your district."

"*I* could do that."

"Not necessary. Our job. . . . Race?" She met his eyes over her bifocals.

"White . . . of course." As soon as it was out of his mouth he realized his grave error in appending the "of course." But the woman, the damn virago, he said to himself, had thrown him off. He had expected name, address, telephone to come first. He should have let *white* stand boldly. There was equivocation. And she immediately caught on. The lie colored his face more deeply.

"Are you sure?"

"Yes, quite sure." Clare felt her stomach twist. Boy barreled on. "My grandfather—"

"And your grandmother, Mr. Savage? Are we to hear of your entire family tree—slave and free?" The specialist smirked at her rhyme.

She did not wait for his reply.

"Well." She smiled at Clare, the first time she had addressed her. "You see"—she turned to Boy—"I am familiar with you island people. My husband and I vacation in Montego Bay occasionally."

This woman acted as if she had been hired by the government to track down Savages trying to pass for white.

"My family is one of the oldest families—"

"And your wife's family, Mr. Savage?"

"My wife and I are separated." Silly declaration. The first time he had admitted his changed state, but senseless in this context. Would Kitty's blood now be erased?

"Mr. Savage, please." A new sternness was in the woman's voice. She was through with his games. Her time was valuable. "Mr. Savage, my husband is a physician. One of the very few Christian doctors left in this city, if you know what I mean."

"Oh, yes. Yes, I do." Boy nodded eagerly. Common ground?

"As such he has had to meet *them* more than halfway. He works for the public health service. In charge of maintaining the obstetrical well-being of Spanish-speaking women in his care." The euphemisms confused her audience. "He is a very witty man. Do you know what he would call you?"

"No," Boy responded, having no idea what was coming next.

"He would call you white chocolate. . . . I mean, have you ever seen a child's expression when he finds a white chocolate bunny in his Easter basket? He simply doesn't understand . . . he thinks it strange. I do not want to be cruel, Mr. Savage, but we have no room for lies in our system. No place for in-betweens."

Time passes. Monday. September 16, 1963. Adjusted to America after a fashion, the girl Clare sits in a green room with red geraniums on the windowsill. Dark green shades flap against the glass. Her father calls this their adopted country. They have lived here for three years. Time passes. Her mother continues to write but her letters hold no resonance—she "keeps in touch." The cotta remains intact. The two sides stand off. Boy suggests that he and his elder daughter may pay a visit. Yes, Kitty writes, that would be a nice thing. Let me know when and I will arrange a place for you to stay. But, he responds, money is short. They will visit as soon as he can make the fare and buy presents for everyone. Hesitation. What *is* he afraid of?

There is quiet until the next exchange. The two maintain a grace of connection—neither expects things to change.

Boy takes up golf. Trades in the '52 Plymouth for a '61 Chevy. Christmas gifts fly to Mountainview Gardens—unaccompanied. Now he sells televisions in the appliance department of Abraham & Straus. A lot of people seem to have credit—business is good.

Through all this—this new life—he counsels his daughter on invisibility and secrets. Self-effacement. Blending in. The uses of camouflage.

September 16, 1963. The girl Clare sits on a high stool in front of her homeroom, chosen by Mrs. Douglass, a Black woman from Americus, Georgia, to read the morning paper to the class. Mrs. Douglass believes in keeping her students informed. Today there is a story which should have caused the sun to eclipse the earth—something . . . something in the heavens should have objected.

In thick dark letters, stark: SUNDAY SCHOOL BOMBED—next line, smaller print: FOUR CHILDREN DEAD. A picture accompanies the letters. More pictures inside, they promise. A stained-glass window. Fragments of images dangle from its leaden boundaries. The face of Jesus is ruined. Dark space where the bomb has torn it off. His hands and crook intact. The legend of the window—willing workers—half there, half absent. Clare reads the text, the names, the ages attached to the names. She monotonizes her voice for she is afraid of being moved—and this news has brought her dangerously close. She is afraid of embarrassing herself in front of this class of children who fidget as she speaks.

"Addie Mae Collins, 14; Denise McNair, 11; Carole Robertson, 14; Cynthia Wesley, 14."

She is able to hold two things in her head at the same time. To read fluently while her mind is tracing something else. She has a chemistry quiz that morning and reviews, as she reads, the elements in the periodic table—dissolving the immediate like someone in solitary. First column: Hydrogen, H; Lithium, Li; Sodium, Na; Potassium, K. But she is troubled. Her mind recites, of its own accord: Hydrogen, 14; Lithium, 11; Sodium, 14; Potassium, 14. She has already forgotten the names, but the ages persist. She is older than all of them.

Her voice reads on.

"The Sunday School lesson that morning was 'Love thy neighbor.' It was in the middle of the lesson that witnesses heard a car slow down outside the Sixteenth-Street Baptist Church. Witnesses report that there was a distinct silence, followed by a rush of air, then a deafening explosion. In addition to the four dead, there are twenty-one injured. A man standing in the rubble of the hundred-year-old church was heard to scream, 'Love them? Love them? I hate them!' "

Clare's voice stopped. *How could he not?* The class was still in motion. *Had they not heard?* Passing notes. Copying homework. Aligning their books on their desktops spine to spine. She glanced at Mrs. Douglass, head up and down as she kept busy with her Delaney cards, recording attendance by sight. There was no rush of air in the room. No explosion. Clare folded the newspaper and returned it to the teacher's desk. She muttered, "I'm sorry," the phrase she had been taught for people bereft, and felt foolish. Unable to go further.

The next morning, on her way to school, she put a nickel in the blind man's plastic dish at the mouth of the subway and picked up a copy of the *News*. On the front page was the picture she needed to see. A girl in a coffin, open. Girl, coffin, platform, all draped in a fine white cotton, like a delicate mosquito netting protecting her from the tiny marauders of a tropical night. A curtain to protect onlookers from the damage. The veiled girl identified in the caption as "one of the victims of Sunday's bombing." There she was—still and whole. As if sleeping, the undertaker might have advertised. Clare wondered what the veil hid, then was ashamed for wondering, confusing the sleeping pose with resting in peace. She cut the picture from the paper and put it in a celluloid pocket in her wallet—to glance at it even when they buried the President and she and her father watched the television nonstop for three days.

It was during that strange weekend in November that her father caught her glancing at the picture of the dead girl. He asked her what was keeping her attention so. She replied, "Nothing." Thinking perhaps a movie star was stealing her mind from American history in the making, he demanded to see the picture. She held her wallet toward his chair. They came to grief over it.

"Girl, do you want to labor forever as an outsider?"

"I don't know, Daddy."

"You are too much like your mother for your own good." His voice was ragged, sharp. "You are an American now. You need to realize what that means." He slid the picture from the celluloid, casually folding it into his shirt pocket. "This is for the best," he told her, in a softer voice. "You must not ponder these things so. We are not to judge this country . . . they give us a home. Your mother could never understand that . . . she blamed the whole place for a few ignorant people . . . that's why we lost her."

A soldier at Arlington sounded taps as Boy spoke. He turned from his daughter as his eyes misted.

It did not matter that the picture was gone—it was in her mind. Connecting her with her absent mother.

The picture, and what it represented, like the meeting with the woman principal, the departure of Kitty, encircled a subject which became taboo between father and daughter.

Should a newscast refer to the "burgeoning civil rights movement," her father took care to distract her, and himself, with talk of something else. Not realizing his daughter could hold two things in her mind at once.

When Kitty Freeman Savage died, her brother Frederick telephoned her husband in America, barely able to contain the bitterness in his voice. Then he buried his sister in Kingston, in a cemetery which held no history for her family—burial in her mother's ground was not a question. The ties had been broken. The land was ruinate.

Clare returned home from school—she was a sophomore in college by that time, working three evenings and all day Saturday at Abraham & Straus, a position achieved because of her father's expertise in sales. She returned that particular evening to her father's weeping. He held a glass into which he stared. "Your mother is gone," he told his daughter.

At first Clare thought he was confused—reliving Kitty's departure of five years before. Then he raised his red-rimmed eyes at her and she knew. Just like that. "How?" she asked. She did not cry.

"Your uncle said a brain hemorrhage in the night. . . . He said she had been suffering from headaches. . . . They asked her to see a doctor . . . begged, he said . . . to go to Miami if necessary . . . but she wouldn't leave. . . . Your mother was the soul of stubbornness." He sat before his daughter, thinking, Yes, that was it, Kitty brought it on herself.

In her last letters to them nothing had been said to indicate to them she was suffering. "I am glad you are studying," she wrote a P.S. to her elder daughter. "I hope someday you make something of yourself, and someday help your people." A reminder, daughter—never forget who your people are. Your responsibilities lie beyond me, beyond yourself. There is a space between who you are and who you will become. Fill it.

This death came without warning. No dogs howled. Had they done so, the daughter would not have sensed the significance of their noise.

She woke at twenty to find herself a motherless child—plainly.

What would her mother think of her on this truck? Of the task ahead of all of them? Could she love her for it?

At breakfast the morning after the news arrived, Boy pressed her. "Have you cried for your mother yet?" He spoke behind eyes newly wet.

"No." Her voice did not break.

In a sudden he was on her. "You callous little bitch. I suppose you have more feeling for niggers than for your own mother." Out it slid. The fury he had been holding in him escaped—the cause of his loss. Again, he aligned his daughter with his wife, who had abandoned him to strangers and died without a word.

Clare breathed deep, looked full into his furious face. "My mother was a nigger"—speaking the word at him.

His five long fingers came at her, as she had expected, marking her cheekbone, making her weep in shock.

"And so am I," she added, softly.

She left the table to splash cold water on her face and get away from him for a moment. When she returned, he spoke to her as if nothing had passed between them, as if they had just joined one another at breakfast. He spoke to her without enthusiasm. "Your sister will be coming here."

And so she did. Speaking her mother's language, while Clare spoke her father's adopted tongue. One daughter raised in captivity, the other in the wild—so it seemed to Clare. Jennie came to them as to two strangers.

For her Kitty was vivid. They had slept in the same room in Mountainview Gardens, in the shadow of Wareika Hill. She had heard her mother cry out, "Jesus! Tek me now!" She was not able to tell these people about it. She sensed that they envied her, that they did not know what to do with her. She existed in an afterlife where her mother surrounded her; she thought her mother could see her every move. Her dreams told her that.

"Did she leave anything behind?" Clare questioned the bluefoot sitting across from her.

"What you mean? She lef' me."

"No. Did she leave anything behind? I would like to have something of hers . . . a keepsake."

"Only this ring." Jennie lifted the wedding band for Clare to see. It hung around her neck on a length of string.

"Did she wear that?"

"Yes. From time to time."

"You better not let him see it; he'll take it for himself."

"Him will have to cut me to get it."

Silence. Then Clare spoke again, tentatively posing the one question she needed answered.

"Did she ever say why she left?"

The girl just stared at the ring around her neck.

"Why she left this place so suddenly? I know she couldn't stand it . . . could not make herself at home . . . and she had just lost Grandma . . . but did she ever say why she didn't take me as well?"

The girl spoke without looking at her sister. "One time she say she feel you would prosper here. She say is because you favor backra, and fe you Daddy. Don't feel bad, man."

Silence again. Clare fought herself, not wanting to weep in front of this girl, who meant well by advising her not to regret their mother's choice, as foolish as that was.

"What ever happened to Grandma's place?"

"Oh, it all overgrown by now. Rat live there. None of the family want to business wid it. It possess itself."

"You ever visit it?"

"Few time we go down fe mango season, and fe drink and wash wid de water. She say is de purest water in de world dat."

The years with her mother in the sun had rendered the

105

younger sister dead-gold. Clare struggled within her city skin, birthright gone paler, an image of the river with her mother almost breaking her heart.

She left Jennie to her wanderings in the city. Left Boy to his newfound love—not his rediscovered daughter but an Italian-American widow who sold cosmetics on the main floor of A&S. The woman tried to be kind to Jennie, silently wondering when she would lose her tan, bringing her vials of sample scents, tubes of sample lipsticks, discouraging the girl when she returned from suspicious places with strange victuals. It upset her father too much, the woman told her, to smell curried goat after all this time.

As soon as she finished school, Clare left home. She borrowed money from her mother's brother Frederick, pledging to repay him, took a student fare to London, and began to explore. Nothing held her.

The truck stopped briefly at a settlement outside of Accompong Town. An old man approached the truck and spoke briefly with the driver. Others—people of the bloodlines of the Maroons—came out of their small houses and gathered around NO TELEPHONE TO HEAVEN. They smiled in welcome of the people in the truck-back, several women passing cups of sorrel and ginger cooled with a block of ice amongst the soldiers. The soldiers unloaded the food they carried and handed over these provisions to the people. The old man squatted, sucking on the stem of his chalice, and gave directions in exchange—in Coromantee, a tongue barely alive.

A tongue she could not speak. She who was educated in several tongues, the mastery of which should have kept her from that truck and stifled her longing to know Coromantee.

5

ET IN
ARCADIA EGO

...The child turned round
And looked up piteous in the mother's face

. . . .

"Oh, mother!" then, with desperate glance to heaven,
"God, free me from my mother," she shrieked out,
"These mothers are too dreadful."

—ELIZABETH BARRETT BROWNING, "Aurora Leigh"

Clare Savage began her life-alone. Choosing London with the logic of a creole. This was the mother-country. The country by whose grace her people existed in the first place. Her place could be here. America behind her, way-station. This was natural.

She was not prepared for the dark women in saris cleaning the toilets at Heathrow. She tried to put them from her mind. Replacing them with lessons from St. Catherine's School for Girls, coming back at her, the expatriate women and light natives trying their best to civilize her and other girls like her. Trained to possess them at impressionable ages. Come out of the trees, girls, take those bones out of your hair. Poor teachers. Had they done wrong?

Even after high school and college in America their lessons stuck in Clare's head. She could still conjure the monarchs in consecutive order, faces and names, consorts and regents, offspring and stillbirth, and some nights, when sleep was distant, she would pass them across her inner eye. Divorced, beheaded, died. Divorced, beheaded, survived. Gloriana.

None had called her white chocolate. None had blown children apart in church.

If reciting the monarchs failed to bring sleep, she would draw the world map in her brain, drenching those sections in red which contained the Empire, now Commonwealth. Or recite the text of Tennyson's "Lady of Shalott" and remember how the girls used to giggle when the Lady cried, "The curse is come upon me!" Long time ago. There was comfort in these acts of memory. Familiarity. Connection.

Her uncle had written her when he sent the money she requested: her mother had spoken of her often, and he hoped she would put the money toward bettering herself. England, he assured her, was the true place for her now. America he called crude, and took the opportunity in his letter wrapped around a check to blame her father for the death of her mother in his stubborn devotion to that nation. "Well, my dear, like to like, as they say, crude to crude." She flinched; Boy was still her father. Her uncle continued, saying Jamaica was not the place for her either—she had not mentioned that option to him; it had not occurred to her. Her mother's death was fresh, her own voice unsteady. No, he said to this niece he had last seen some years before, no need to bury yourself there. You have a chance to leave that narrow little island behind you—distancing himself in his phrasing from the place in which he wrote. He sounded a familiar refrain; by *chance* he meant light skin. There was no escaping it. He remembered how of all the cousins her skin was most subject to burn, while her sister only kept darkening. The two girls were, in his words, "river and sea." The matter of skin was central to his thinking. He was a member of his group. The letter ended with an invitation to "visit your Aunt Violet and myself on your holiday—life spare and God willing."

She wrote him deepest thanks—on a postcard with the

rounded becrowned little lady who meant so much to them—
and said, Yes, she would visit them on her holiday, perhaps
at Christmastime.

She spent the next few years in observance of this
country she had been taught to call Mother.

She found herself in a dim bed-sitting room in Notting
Hill—she took the first place she looked at. She opened a
heavy door into a dark hall, walls covered on each side in
deep-red wildly floral paper. Ugly and new, it would bracket
the hall for years. The landlady, a gaunt woman with a smile
at once patronizing and ingratiating, led her to a room at
the top of the house, commenting in her garish voice about
the quality of the tenants. Cyprus, Nigeria, Australia, Leeds—
"all students, mind you. All except the lady in five, who
writes letters to herself, poor dear. Intimate letters"—she
clucked—"signed 'Victoria Cross.' Fancy." Clare did not ask
the landlady how she knew this.

The woman spread her arm to introduce the room to
Clare. Iron bed, oak wardrobe, table and two chairs, and hot
plate and sink. Next to the sink were a few shelves which
held plates and cups. A shilling-fire was set into one wall in
the room—the only real piece of brightness.

"I can't tell you how many times I have had to take a
knife to that thing," the landlady told her, referring to the
shilling-meter. "All manner of strange currency has jammed
her." Clare acknowledged the warning with a nod, looking
at the walls striped gray and pink and yellow, against a crim-
son rug. All darkening.

She paid the woman eight pounds and took up residence. From a small shop at the corner she bought the ingredients for each evening meal, which she did not vary.
Eggs, cheese, and small tomatoes mixed into an omelet. She
drank instant Nescafé with milk, the milk poured from a
container in the shape of a trapezoid. The trapezoid promised that were the milk unopened it could keep for five
months—the trapezoid held space without matter, except for
the molecules of milk.

She settled into living in this small room. Filling her time with walks, museums, films, books. She walked the Portobello Road on Saturday mornings. She looked at the various plunder in the stalls—old china plates and old family jewelry. She thought of her mother's wedding ring. She tried to limit evocations of her mother. She turned to the cheap shoes and cheap sweaters. *And cheap tin trays* sounded in her head. Pyramids of tinned goods.

She noticed—without effort—how the English sellers spoke to the colored buyers, native dress partly hidden by shabby winter coats. Kente cloth and silver bangles incongruous in the gray cold. She turned from her observation to face a display of golliwogs, grotesquerie, and remembered suddenly how her mother had torn a book in half when Clare was six or so. *Little Black Sambo,* given her by an auntie. She had not thought of that book in years and years, nor of the fury she felt at her mother's destructiveness.

Had the act been explained to her? She could not say.

One morning a brooch caught her eye. A badge more than a brooch, shaped like a shield, of red and blue cloisonné, it had the Cross of Lorraine on the front of it, along with the word *Résistez.* She did not buy it because she did not want to pay the price—she had to conserve her money, she told herself—and couldn't bring herself to bargain with the seller, knowing that her half-American, half-Jamaican intonation would draw comments and make her conspicuous, the last thing she wanted.

There was something about the brooch which drew her to it, an absoluteness. The sense of cause—clear-cut, heroic—one she could not join. *I will dare, and dare, and dare, until I die*—she remembered from St. Catherine's the words of St. Joan, for she had belonged to the house of Arc. She only stopped gazing at the badge when the seller asked if he could be of help. She shook her head and moved off. Another woman, tribal scars cutting diagonally across her cheeks, took Clare's place.

She thought often about the badge the next week. She returned Saturday to claim it. Of course it had been sold. Foolishly, she thought, she added it to her list of regrets, which she kept against herself. That she had not bucked her father and joined a demonstration decrying the murder of Dr. King. That she was not as dark as her sister, mother. That she allowed the one to become confused with the other, and so lessen her.

Résistez. What else was there? Now, on this truck taking her higher—toward the culmination of her journey—she might think of Lorraine. Her cross. Her burden of dream. Deferred. *I ain't got long to stay here.* Yes, baby girl.

On Sundays the museums were free of charge. She wandered around them after reading the *Observer.* She moved between the National Gallery, the Tate, the British Museum. She collected impressions.

On sunny days she tended to the British Museum, which was almost unbearably gloomy on rainy ones. In rain its heaviness overwhelmed her—inside and out. The sooted expanse of the exterior, dark porch, laconic guards checking for Irish explosives, poking through knapsacks, carrier bags, sparing no one. The dripping insides as girl guides and boy scouts and Sunday-attired families and old-age pensioners traipsed past slashes in the stone, fragments of Amazons fighting to the death, great charter of the barons—basis, so read the legend, of the democratic system. Please do not forget where you are. Hauling their umbrellas and raincoats past the vast accumulation. Traces of desert peoples. People of the rainforest. People touched by sun. People who worshiped fire. People lit by a purple light. People who invented the compass. People who returned as elephants. People who made paper. People who married their sisters. People who danced in temples. People who made war with fine stones. People who knew kindness. Chaos. Their traces collided here. Did spirits collect in these rooms? She did not think how all of this had come to be. She took note of the Assyrian lions, the Egyptian coffin paintings, the Hittite drinking goblets.

On most rainy, bone-wet Sunday afternoons, Clare went to the National or the Tate. Standing before the yellows and reds and blues of Turner, reality turning to a fog of color, as Parliament burned or Dido built Carthage or Rain and Steam and Speed slashed the canvas, rushing.

In a corner of the Tate, unto itself, stood a slate sculpture. Two figures. Menhirs. Clean and unencumbered. Single standing stones, imitators of the guardians of the far past. Side by side as if lovers. The ancient circles, lines, telling time. She touched the open spaces slit into the stone. Ran a finger over one lip. Was reprimanded. "Mind, miss. Mind," a guard whispered at her. She left the corridor and bought a postcard of the sculpture and set it on the mantelpiece over her fire.

Time passed. Slid, really. The days, with her museum visits, public lectures, browsing in bookshops, sitting in striped sling chairs, reading *Coming Up for Air* in Green Park, matinees of *Death in Venice* and *The Ruling Class*, watching, watching people pedaling swan boats, a band in uniform, furious ducks. She traced the mother-country, recognizing things she had been taught, surprised by others. She read the pronouncements of Enoch Powell, classics scholar.

The days went by. The nights were more difficult.

One evening she heard the noise of a black taxicab pulling up outside, the soft hum of the engine and dull slam of the door as someone emerged. The downstairs bell sounded, as she knew it would, and she was certain the visitor was for her, now ascending the stairs to her room, having been passed by the landlady. Perhaps carrying presents. Surely from a long way away. So certain was she, and so eager, she opened the door to her room and stood at the top of the flight, waiting to greet her visitor, someone who knew her. At the bottom of the stairs, feet planted on the fake Persian runner, the landlady was informing an African student she was full up. Telling him he might try the house at the corner. Clare immediately retreated to her room and lay down on the bed. Frightened of her certainty. What if the landlady had seen her?

She glanced around the room, trying to fix herself in its realness. Where had the feeling come from? She stood and walked over to the fire, running her hand along the hardness of the mantel, then kneeling to make the heat redden her face. When the warmth became too much, she rose and went to the sink, running cold water into her cupped hands and splashing it over her cheeks and eyelids.

She did these things automatically—extending herself into the dimensions of the room. This was here. Now. Its solidity, heat, liquid. She walked back and forth across the floor trying to think clearly.

Whom had she awaited? Who was there in the world to seek her out in this room?

No one. Not really.

Unless it was the woman on the tube. A reasonable possibility presented itself in her mind. She grabbed it. The day before she had given a light to the woman sitting next to her on the tube. The two had chatted and the woman asked her to be her guest at the ballet that evening. Margot Fonteyn was dancing, the woman said. Clare fled.

Had she expected the woman to seek her out? Did she want this? A simple want next to the want she felt. Lying on the bed now, calmed, she rehearsed the incident on the tube, finally dismissing the woman. Not with presents. Not from far away. They had not even exchanged names.

She picked up the book beside her. *Jane Eyre.* Used, bought recently in a bookshop in Camden Passage, shabby nineteenth-century binding, pages bearing vague stains, fingered, smoothed. She opened the book to the place she left it when the taxicab pulled up.

"My daughter, flee temptation."

"Mother, I will," Jane responded, as the moon turned to woman.

The fiction had tricked her. Drawn her in so that she became Jane.

Yes. The parallels were there. Was she not heroic Jane? Betrayed. Left to wander. Solitary. Motherless. Yes, and with no relations to speak of except an uncle across the water. She occupied her mind.

Comforted for a time, she came to. Then, with a sharpness, reprimanded herself. No, she told herself. No, she could not be Jane. Small and pale. English. No, she paused. No, my girl, try Bertha. Wild-maned Bertha. Clare thought of her father. Forever after her to train her hair. His visions of orderly pageboy. Coming home from work with something called Tame. She refused it; he called her Medusa. Do you intend to turn men to stone, daughter? She held to her curls, which turned kinks in the damp of London. Beloved racial characteristic. Her only sign, except for dark spaces here and there where melanin touched her. Yes, Bertha was closer the mark. Captive. Ragôut. Mixture. Confused. Jamaican. Caliban. Carib. Cannibal. Cimarron. All Bertha. All Clare.

She closed her eyes. Closed the book over her index finger.

If the dead speak to you in a dream it means you will soon be amongst them. Was this her grandmother's wisdom? Her mother was standing next to the bed, looking down at her daughter. Making as if to speak. Then drawing her hand across her mouth as if to wipe away her words.

Clare was unable to shake her longing when she woke. She spent the next three days watching for black taxicabs and listening for them when it became dark. No one came.

When she imagined the noise of a cab, one night soon after her vigil ended, imagined someone standing in the street gently calling her name, when she could not dismiss this by touching her surroundings—she became terrified and knew she must end her solitude. Her aloneness was catching up with her; that was all.

She took herself to High Holborn the next morning and declared herself a legal resident, showing them a savings

116

book with the remains of her uncle's money, convincing them she would not sponge off the mother-country. The old lady had enough to contend with, without another Jamaican arriving unannounced, expecting to be clasped to her shrinking bosom.

"Then again, you're not at all like our Jamaicans, are you."

Clare nodded at this exemption, hoping the people in line behind her had not heard.

After securing her status, she walked to the Senate House of the University of London and, brushing aside a suggestion that she register at the School of Oriental and African Studies, applied to an institute to study the artifacts of a small group of people who lived several hundred years before. People, it was said, who adored beauty.

Her transcripts were sent for; she was accepted.

She began to better herself.

This suited her for a time. Study. Dreams and images. Refuge. Rivalry of nature. Balance. Harmony. None enters here unless he is a geometer. Mnemonics. Order from chaos. Theater of the world. Structure. Art. Illusion. Original texts. She needed this—yes. Her head filled. Shower of gold. Split brow of Zeus. Calumny of Apelles. Splendor of tombs. Sacred and profane love. Christ's agony, besides. Piero's resurrection.

Form/Content. Active/Contemplative. Perspective. Vanishing point. Line/Circle. Agape/Eros. Aphrodite Urania/ Aphrodite Pandemos. Philosopher's stone. She sought the death of Actaeon from Ovid into Titian. The rape of Leda from Sappho into Michelangelo. Read *Elegantiae. Timaeus. Profugiorum ab Aerumna.* She was praised for the way she analyzed Aristotle's definition of *place* in the *Physics.* Each thing exists in place. Each thing is described by place. Would this new knowledge have pleased her mother? She did not know.

People admired her mind and implied her good fortune in escaping the brain damage common to creoles. Not in so many words. Tongues came back to her. Latin—all the way from St. Catherine's, where she had won a prize. French—she read the poetry of Louise Labé and the letters of Catherine de Médicis. Spanish—*La Celestina* and *La Vida Es Sueño*. She threw herself into Italian and German. These things gave her comfort—strangely. The winged soul of *Phaedrus* on a medallion by Donatello. The vision of Leonardo releasing birds bought in the marketplace. The nun who concealed her life in the webbing of her chair—unweaving and reweaving in secret.

When she read how Marguerite de Navarre sat by the bedside of a dying friend to detect the exact instant the soul departed the body, she wept.

After a time at the institute, she accepted her Uncle Frederick's invitation to Kingston and attended the party at Buster Said's house, where she met Paul H., and Harry/Harriet comforted her.

She did not visit her mother's grave. Did not ask after it. Her mother's name was barely spoken except when Aunt Violet commented to some friends gathered for high tea, pouring the blind earl pattern, that Clare's face was the dead-stamp of Kitty, lightening her sister-in-law in death.

The aunt and uncle asked for news of Boy and Jennie, politely—really wanting to let sleeping dogs lie—and nodded but did not speak when Clare told them her father and sister seemed fine, although she barely heard from either one. She preferred when the relatives asked after her studies, obviously impressed by them, as if she could set her paternity right by her action alone. As if to say, See, my father is really not so bad—else now could I be as I am? But the response of her aunt and uncle was of no comfort. Yes, they said to her, you are the daughter of your mother, not that rascal in America. Accomplishment must flow from their side.

Aunt Violet shifted the subject; she was looking at some property in Manor Plaza, not far from their condominium. It would be ideal for an antique shop. She asked that Clare consider joining her in business when she had done with her studies.

Violet and Frederick had sold their house in Barbican some months before and moved into an apartment where things were safer. They told her the reason. The ruffians were preying on people of substance more and more—wuthless brutes, lazy and idle. Now—with the murder of Charles and his lovely family—they congratulated themselves on their good sense. Still, there was room for her in the apartment should she want to stop with them on her return. It would be nice to have a young person in residence, they said. Their son was working at the Revere excavation near Maggotty; their daughter had a family of her own in Toronto. Besides, a young girl had no business on her own; surely she didn't intend to spend more time than necessary in damp old England.

She would think about it, she said. Think about the antique shop and about living in their home. You have been generous to me, I realize that. I realize that I owe you something. Nonsense, Violet said, as if to sweep Clare's obligation aside, you are family, after all.

Below, around the swimming pool at the center of the building complex, children were gathering in costume, dressed as Santa's elves, to sing carols. Their voices floated up to the balcony, and Clare asked if they were the children of residents—grateful for a diversion to a conversation that had begun to weigh on her.

"Oh, no, mi dear," her uncle responded, "they are children from the Wortley Home, here to celebrate the Christmas . . . foundlings, you know."

She was confused. Orphans, foundlings, abandoned babies, fatherless children, little wanderers, were no novelty to the island, of course. And Clare knew that. She remembered how her father, as they left Kingston for her grandmother's place in St. Elizabeth, long time ago, how her father had avoided passing Trench Town, Denham Town, the Dungle. How, when he could not avoid that passage, due to detour, rain, accident, the children swarmed around the car, beating the hood, and she felt shamed. But these children below her were not the same children at all. Even from a distance she could make out their lightness, was startled by it—this thing that in Jamaica was significant of origin, expressive of expectation. Some sprouted blond from under their pointed caps. Violet noticed Clare's fascination. "Outside children, from some of the finest families in Jamaica," she explained with a quaint pride. "It's a lovely place, the home. The children are well cared for," she continued at Clare's back, her niece still turned, looking down at the well-maintained, costumed children.

"We should go down, for the residents have organized a little celebration and we are to distribute stockings to the poor little souls."

So Clare found herself beside a swimming pool, two days after the murder, among children who wore red tunics, belled caps and shoes, and had no people to speak of. The children were thrilled at the table, holding cakes and ices and a giant crystal punch bowl of sorrel, the national Christmas drink. "I see Mrs. Silvera has put her best foot forward," Violet muttered.

One Miss Baxter was the guardian of the children, and Violet appeared to know her, bustling Clare toward the woman to shake her hand and introduce her to "my niece who is at university in London, Frederick's sister's girl." Clare spoke briefly with the woman, not at all able to ask her the questions in her mind. Why are these children in your care? Where are their mothers? Has time stopped? Instead, she took herself off to the side of the pool and sat under the twilight on a chair patterned with hibiscus. She watched as the children received their stockings. She fought tears, but could not stave them off, and was grateful for the darkness falling fast around them. Jesus! What a miserable place this is.

"Now, if they had *any* sense of irony, or history, they would call this place Triangle Trade and be done with it.

The tourists them would never get the joke . . . them would probably think it some sort of sailor's preference back then." Harry/Harriet smiled at Clare, his spangled eyelids glistening red, gold, green in the candlelight. The candle set in a brass ship's lantern, part of the mood of the place. They were in a nightclub at the Pegasus, tables around them filled with coconut husks and hollowed pineapples and pale visitors. The surroundings intended to suggest a galleon on the Spanish Main. Their table an upturned barrel with XXX painted on the side, fake doubloons and pieces of eight set into its top.

For Clare's sake, Harry/Harriet wore a proper dinner jacket, but his face bespoke his usual brave, glamorous self. "Of course, if they were really imaginative, girlfriend, they would hang some whips and chains on the walls, dress the waiters in loincloths, have the barmaid bare her breasts, and call the whole mess the Middle Passage . . . no; No, man . . . too cold. Sorry, these places bring out the worst in me . . . especially since I know I am more welcome here than I would be in a rumshop at Matilda's Corner." He paused. "Our homeland is turned to stage set too much."

The word *homeland* startled Clare. Still, that is what it was. Quiet between them. Harry/Harriet tried to lighten the mood. "I hear a lot of dem back den was on the queerish side . . . is true . . . or is a piece of battyman labrish?"

"Back when?"

"The time you study."

"Oh . . . yes, labrish, but also true-true." Her twang was coming back, rapidly, in Harry/Harriet's presence, voice breaking the taboo of speaking bad. Discouraged among her people.

"Now that might make studying even tolerable . . . at least for some of us, girlfriend."

Clare spun a plastic dagger in her drink, chasing a wedge of lime, then spearing it at the bottom of the glass.

"Tell me something, you ever been tempted?" He raised a meticulously shaped eyebrow as if to mock his question.

"Tempted by what?" she asked, knowing full well what he was asking her.

"Pussy, sweetness . . . loving your own kind."

"Jesus, Harry! Sometimes you are too much." She was annoyed that the question made her uncomfortable and answered her friend too sharply.

"And here I thought we was girlfriends . . . company," Harry/Harriet pushed out his tinted bottom lip as if to make to cry.

Clare couldn't help but smile, but the sharpness remained. "Harry, is what shade of lipstick that? I think it's a bit outré . . . even for you."

"I say, I say . . . coo ya . . . de island-pickney speak French. The tongue of tongues. Tu connais Baby Doc, chérie?"

"Very funny."

"Look, darling, I felt especially colorful tonight. And given the fact that I draped myself in this drab garb, without so much as an earring to recommend me, for your sake, you might be more appreciative . . . or at least kinder."

"I'm sorry. Truly. But, no, I don't think I have been tempted. Unless you count my own—pussy, that is, not kind."

"What a rude girlfriend it is!" Harry/Harriet expressed fake shock by dabbing at his forehead with his cocktail napkin, Captain Blood, or some such icon, prancing amid a confusion of palm trees under a full moon. He composed himself elaborately and went on. "Too bad, darling. But if you ever change your mind, I know a marvelous woman. Older. Dashing. With endless breasts. From one of the finest families of Jamaica, as your auntie might say."

"You?"

"Don't be bizarre . . . but thanks. Or is tease you tease? No, a woman . . . oh, never mind. Just think of me as a corrupter of youth . . . like Socrates. Besides, sweetness, we are the same age."

Clare ignored the last observation; of course she had been teasing, wanting to dismiss the subject.

"Is where you read Plato?"

"Ah, girlfriend is pleased we can switch to book." Their eyes met, with understanding. Harry/Harriet continued. "Nuh read him at Calabar? When I was schoolbwai. You forget how them drill us in them labrish? De master mek us read about five of dem dialogue. . . . Teaching us to be gentlemen . . . disdaining us all the while."

"And what did you think? About the dialogues, I mean."

"Dem nuh tell us what to think? But, even so . . . even with them talk about golden age this and Platonic love that, I couldn't . . . my twelve-year-old self couldn't comprehend why it so gold if dem keep slave . . . if dem women lock up so. Why Jamaica den nuh golden, eh?"

"You didn't tell the master this?"

"I did."

"And?"

"And him was sharp. Him tell me since me is battyman-in-training, me should cleave to Plato. And him say that Jamaica is paradise, wasted on the likes of we. And the rest of the class laugh."

"What did you do?"

"I don't remember. It was not the first time they held me to ridicule . . . hardly . . . nor the last . . . but I never learn. Not this lickle Black bwai."

"Harry, is how you know Jamaica not golden?"

"Cyaan live on this island and not understand how it work, how the world work. Cyaan pass the Dungle, cyaan smell the Dungle, and not know this island is the real world . . . in the worst way. Even if you were to live your entire life on this island, and never see nor smell the Dungle, nuh mus' know it there? It nuh stand as warning for all a we— no matter how light? how bright? how much of dem labrish we master? Nuh mus' question?"

"I remember once . . . long time . . . we passed through Trench Town," Clare said, "and I saw a pregnant woman squatting in the gutter . . . I was about twelve, I think. Her bowed head when she spied the car of backra people—for to her we were *backra* people . . . my father said something, I don't recall. My mother made him stop the car and went over to the woman, putting some money on the pavement next to her. The woman raised her head to look at my mother . . . my mother went to put her hand on the woman's shoulder, then pulled back suddenly . . . as if a force field separated them."

"Which of course it did . . . still does."

Clare looked past her friend to the dance floor, fighting emotion.

"Yes. Not the dirt, nor the smell of the woman. . . . My mother returned to the car, eyes wet. She seemed . . . I don't know. . . . I remember I asked what was wrong . . . no one said a word . . . we continued in silence . . . all the way to St. Elizabeth . . . with my father occasionally testing the waters . . . and my mother not responding."

"Indeed, mi love, indeed."

Clare sipped her drink. "Harry, how were you able to question, to know to question, so early?"

"Don't forget, mi mumma was a maid, and my father, her employer. And dem keep me and let she go. Is how you think she come to bear me?"

"Did you know that when you were a boy?"

"Don't know when I knew . . . but I knew soon enough that in that house I was an odd quantity . . . outside."

"You in touch with your mother?"

"Man, you mus' live inna castle."

"Sometimes I wish I did . . . about five hundred years ago . . . and—" Clare's fantasy was interrupted by the shadow of a large whiteman, cast across their table. In the background the band was playing ancient calypso—"The Big Bamboo." "Pardon me, miss, but my wife and I are visitors to your island and wondered if you and your friend—"

> *The Big Bamboo grows straight and tall*
> *The Big Bamboo pleases one and all . . .*

Clare said nothing. The man turned to face Harry/Harriet for the first time. Barely concealing his shock at the man/woman's painted visage. Clare would have sworn Harry/Harriet twinkled his eyelids for the man. From a distance, where the visitor had been sitting, only the back of Harry/Harriet's head and his dignified dinner jacket had been visible. "Yes?" Harry/Harriet met the intruder's eyes, demanding he continue . . . or leave. The man turned back to Clare, speaking in hushed tones, as if she were Harry/Harriet's keeper. "I'm terribly sorry . . . ah, to bother you."

Keep away from the Big Bamboo.

"That's perfectly all right"—Clare approximated an Oxbridge accent—"perfectly . . . but you see, my husband"—she paused to let the word sink in—"my husband and I"—Christ! I sound like Elizabeth II giving her Christmas message—"my husband and I are also visitors to this island . . . he is the crown prince of Benin, in Africa, and I am his first wife."

The man stared, color high. Harry/Harriet picked up the joke. "Yes," extending his hand, rising slightly from his seat, only as far as he imagined a prince of Africa would rise to greet a stranger, "I am Prince Badnigga, and this is my consort, Princess Cunnilinga; we are here for the International Festival of Practitioners of Obeah, my dear chap."

The man took Harry/Harriet's hand and bowed slightly. "Obeah?"

"Voo-doo," Clare interjected, pronouncing each syllable as distinctly as possible. "Zombies and the like."

"Oh." The man seemed eager to depart, but Harry/Harriet held on.

"I see you have noticed my eyelids . . . these are the colors of our national flag. . . . At the first sign of manhood each young warrior in our country must do the same . . . like most ancient customs it has a practical basis . . . going back to the days when we devoured our enemies. . . . I mean, we needed the means to distinguish, didn't we?"

Poor man, did he not see their eyes jump with the joke? Afrekete and Anansi. But no, the poor fool, now released, took the whole story back to his table to tell his wife he had spoken with African royalty, and, oh, dear, they are as we feared.

"God, Harry"—Clare dabbed at her eye corners—"what a poor t'ing . . . how he could believe that?"

"Poor t'ing nothing . . . we have given him a story he will tell and tell and tell. The sort of t'ing they all want. Exotic. Af-ri-can. Hot nights and mystery. He will return to him lickle business or town or office or country club where everybody is exactly the same and tell them all. By the time he returns he may have kissed Princess Cunnilinga and advised Prince Badnigga in affairs of state. . . . Jesus! . . . Why them cyaan jus' visit and lef' us be?"

They laughed together, bitterly.

"Last evening," Clare said, "I was at my aunt and uncle. There were some children there, around the swimming pool, from some place called the Wortley Home. You know it?"

"Yes, me know it."

"Licklemos' you could have been one of those children."

"Yes, girlfriend, yes. But better there than Dungle."

"They were dressed in Christmas costume, Santa's elves. Well-behaved. Contained. Opening their stockings carefully, told to take one toy from the stocking and give the rest to the guardian. The whole damn thing made me sad . . . very sad."

"Tell me something . . . you would feel as miserable if you saw darker, dirtier, wilder pickney getting Christmas stocking, being treated to things they had never dreamed of?"

"I'm not sure what you mean."

"I mean it is perhaps *Margaret* you mourn for."

"Perhaps."

"I mean, girlfriend, company, that both sets are cast-offs, and that is always sad, but wasn't your own sadness partly because you didn't expect these light, quiet, clean children to be unwanted? In our system such children are born to be prized, loved; that is at least what we have been taught, no? . . . Why else trace the face, the hair, the knees and elbows, almost at the point of birth?"

126

"All that, yes. But something else too. They, the children from the Wortley Home, seemed almost ghostly to me. Maybe something to do with Aunt Violet describing them as 'outside children' . . . like they belonged to the past."

"But we *are* of the past here. So much of the past that we punish people by flogging them with cat-o'-nine-tails. We expect people to live on cornmeal and dried fish, which was the diet of the slaves. We name hotels Plantation Inn and Sans Souci. . . . A peculiar past. For we have taken the master's past as our own. That is the danger."

Clare nodded, not ready to take on all he had said. "My aunt and uncle have asked me to come to Jamaica after I have finished with school and help Aunt Violet in an antique business she's thinking of starting . . . speaking of the past."

"You think you will?"

"I don't know yet. I'll think about it."

"This place nuh your home? Things can change here, you know."

"I don't know about that at all."

"You cyaan think England is your place."

"Probably not."

"Then, girlfriend, that is the solution. Come home. I'll be here. Come back to us, once your studies are finished. Could help bring us into the present." He smiled at her, then dropped his voice in seriousness. "Jamaica's children have to work to make her change. It will be worthwhile . . . believe me."

"Harry, how come you talk this way when at the party you were going on about dancing in England before the Queen?"

"Oh, man, girlfriend, is nuh what dem expect from me? Nuh jus' give dem what dem expect? Battyman trash. No harm. Our people kind of narrow, poor souls. Foolish sometimes. Cyaan understand the likes of me."

Not many could, she thought to say, but didn't.

"No, man, jus' give dem what dem want. No need to get deep. No need to tell them my asshole was split when I was a bwai by an officer at Up Park Camp—no need a-tall, a-tall." He could feel her unease across the table and worried that he was asking too much of her by telling her this.

Clare spoke softly. "I'm sorry. I didn't know." Feeling but inadequate in her reaction.

A waiter dressed as a buccaneer descended on them at that instant and took Harry/Harriet's order for another piña colada and a fresh rum-and-water. The waiter left. "And no, girlfriend, before you ask, if you intended to ask, or assume, that did not make me the way I am. No, darling, I was born this way, that I know. Not just sun, but sun and moon." (Was he not romancing . . . could someone be born that way . . . wasn't damage intrinsic . . . what do you know about it, eh? what in hell do you know about it?) "Forever following after the maid, the one they hired to replace my mother—Hyacinth, her name—forever after the poor woman, 'Beg you loan me fe you lipstick,' 'Beg you put some Khus Khus on my wrists when you tidy me,' 'Beg you ask dem pierce my ears, and ring them with delicate hoops.' She was sweet with me; kind. No, man, that t'ing didn't make me who I am. Didn't form me in all my complexity. But the man's brutishness made my journey hard, hard. Nearly wilted my full-flower, girlfriend. Ten years old and guilty that a big man in a khaki uniform, braided and bemedaled, in the garrison of Her Majesty, did to me what he did. What else to expect but guilt . . . or shame . . . whiteman, Black bwai."

Harry/Harriet took Clare's hand across the table. The palms were hot, but she held on and didn't pull back.

"Look, girlfriend, I tell you this because I want you to know about me. I trust you with this. You don't have to say a word."

Clare squeezed her friend's hand, feeling almost womanly in her sympathy, her ability to feel for him. "How could he—"

"Easy, mi love. He found me sitting on the steps of the

library one morning, one Saturday. My weekly ration of stories, my contact with the outside world, beside me 'pon the steps. I was waiting for the bus to come. The man came over. Said something about what a sweet lickle t'ing I was . . . except he said 'monkey,' sweet lickle monkey. Afterwards I worried about the books. For I had lost them. I was afraid to return to the library after that, afraid they would punish me for losing the books, or accuse me of teefing dem. Afraid they would tell my father and he would find out what happened. So, for a time, I lost my contact with the outside world."

"That bastard . . . that bastard . . ." Clare whispered; Harry/Harriet went on.

"My parents—that is, my father and my adoptive mother—never found out. Hyacinth, God rest her sweet soul, was at the market in Crossroads, doing the weekly shopping for the family. I was to meet her there; that's why I was waiting for the bus. I managed to walk to the market, afraid to take the bus, hoping against hope that another small Black bwai, even one bleeding and crying, would not be noticed on the streets of Kingston. And I wasn't. Hyacinth took care of me. She hid what happened from my family, who were at their house on the North Coast for a few days. Lucky. She said she was afraid for me, afraid if they found out I would be 'ruined' and turned from son to servant. 'Wunna is on sufferance here,' she told me more than once.

"She undressed me with such a gentleness—carefully, slowly peeling the cloth back from my skin. She bathed me. Brewed roots into a poultice. Made me honey tea. Told me Anansi stories to keep my mind from the pain. She saved me.

"Darling, I know it is hard to listen to all of this; it is hard to tell. I have been tempted in my life to think *symbol*—that what he did to me is but a symbol for what they did to all of us, always bearing in mind that some of us, many of us, also do it to each other. But that's not right. I only suffered what my mother suffered—no more, no less.

129

Not symbol, not allegory, not something in a story or a dialogue by Plato. No, man, I am merely a person who felt the overgrown cock of a big whiteman pierce the asshole of a lickle Black bwai—there it is. That is all there is to it."

"Harry," Clare said, regarding this peculiar little person across the table from her, delicately sipping his piña colada, "Harry, you make me want to love you." She had never said that to anyone before this. She did not spoil her feeling by asking herself "Why?"

The next day they took a drive up the coast road toward St. Thomas, turning right at a dirt road running through a huge canefield. Harry/Harriet trespassing determinedly, telling her this was the most beautiful beach on the island, and the most secluded, and besides, the landlord was an American, absentee. They could swim as girlfriends.

They came to the end of the road, parked, and walked through bush and canetrash to the side of the water, sharing their short trek with lizards and songbirds. Not another human in sight, they spread their towels and picnic on the thin strand—ripe mangoes, meat patties, a bottle of golden rum. "What more do smaddy need?" Harry/Harriet asked her. Clare decided they needed something to mix with the rum. Harry/Harriet said, "Wait a minute, girlfriend," and returned to the Rover. Shortly, he came back with a rifle and a box of shells, and a clean cutlass, loaded down with armaments like a "fairy guerrilla," he said.

"I haven't climbed a coconut tree in donkey's years," he explained to Clare. The green coconuts, shot clean between the fronds, rained around them, thumping and rolling on the sand. Harry/Harriet sliced two open with his cutlass, and they poured rum into the sweet water, the mixture dribbling over them. This was but the beginning. Soon they would be covered with mango juice, salt water, and the spicy oil of the meat. Resting from riding the breakers, warmed by their feast and the sun, they lay side by side under a sky thrilling in its brightness. Touching gently, kissing, tongues entwined, coming to, laughing.

"Girlfriend, tell me something. Do you find me strange?"

Clare looked into her friend's eyes. Mascara and eye shadow washed away by the salt water, the eyes stood out, deep brown. Her own eyes naked, green as the cane behind them. She thought, Of course I find you strange; how could I not? You are a new person to me. At the same time I feel drawn to you. At home with you.

"No, I don't find you strange. No stranger . . . no stranger than I find myself. For we are neither one thing nor the other."

"At the moment, darling, only at the moment."

"What do you mean?"

"I mean the time will come for both of us to choose. For we will have to make the choice. Cast our lot. Cyaan live split. Not in this world."

Clare lay back, shutting her eyelids against the fire of the sun. She thought she could feel the tint of her skin deepening, melanin rising to the occasion. Harry/Harriet continued.

"There is a vast canefield right behind us. Less than ten yards from our blessed bodies is cane. Do you know what went on, what happened along those avenues? In the buildings at the center of the piece? I'm not talking about the new landlord's glass house, or the new sugarworks. I'm talking about the ruins. . . . Licklemos' you could glimpse them, but of course the cane too high. And were we to walk to them, our legs would be sliced fine by the blades of the cane . . . sharp, sharp."

"Yes, I remember," Clare responded, recalling how as a small child famous for her stubbornness she had insisted on walking through her grandmother's cane. She did not get far; her bare legs soon stung and bled—her lips too, for she refused to cry.

"But I have seen them . . . for I come here often," Harry/Harriet went on. "Some of our people, girlfriend . . . some of our ancestors. Now, the slave hospital, that is truly something. Built from limestone and brain coral—held together by molasses, you know. Is what dem use to seal the stones. Were you to see it, you with your English education, you might think it was the wreck of a stately home, for even now, a shell, it is splendid, with its rondels and arches."

"Why a hospital, Harry? Why dem bother?"

"Tek a lot of smaddy fe grow cane, missis. Cyaan have smaddy dying off—not when dem cost so. No, girlfriend. . . . T'ink of de duppy in such a place, eh? Dem nuh mus' crash together in de night . . . ? But, you know, t'ings not so different now. Do you know what happens on this island still? The lives of cutters, of timekeepers? Why? Oh, sweetie, I am sorry to preach, for me know is preach me preach, and you come with me today to have some fun, but is hard, missis. Were we to sleep on this beach we might hear more than the breeze rattling the stalks, and singing through the blades. We might feel more than its warmth. We might hear more than our people celebrating cropover." He took her hand. "Enough . . . enough of this. Harry-gal, you is too morbid. Let us walk up the sand a bit. I know a mangrove swamp nearby where there are plenty-plenty oysters. A few alligators too, but dem nuh bother we."

His words reached Clare through levels of consciousness, as the sun began to burn her salt-caked skin.

On the truck now, standing silently across from her friend, a chill as they climbed further, would she remember the sweetness of oysters, the warm scum of the swamp, the black stalks, water lapping softly against them, stalks casting cool shadows in that afternoon. Standing for what seemed hours, tasting the rawness, naked. Surprising the sea-creature by a stroke of the cutlass, pinpoint end honed against coral, itself alive, as precise as a scalpel. The mix of sweet and salt—they devoured hundreds, and hundreds more remained. Is this the sort of thing she thinks about? The beauty, the wildness of this New World—her point of origin.

Would she remember her answer to her friend's talk of

the canefields, her impatience spoken to herself—And what am I supposed to do about it?

Clare made friends with another student at the institute. A woman recently down from Cambridge, tracing the presence of hats, the significance of color and shape, in the battle scenes of Uccello. Some don's notion of a dissertation subject, she explained. "When he said, 'Why not hats in Uccello?'—I gather a pet curiosity of his—I said, 'Why not codpieces at the court of Henry the Eighth?' and in all seriousness he responded, 'Because the visual depictions leave much to be desired'—pompous old fool.

"Still, it's not as silly as it sounds," the woman—named Liz—continued. "Once you get into it, there is something to it . . . the merchants' obsession with display . . . commerce . . . objects . . . trade routes . . . in Florence in the fifteenth century." She seemed apologetic, unconvinced. "I expect it always goes back to the merchants' obsession with one thing or the other. . . .

"And what are you doing here? Who is your man?"

Clare knew that Liz, with whom she was sharing coffee, unsweetened instant, in the common room, meant by *man* the subject of her own research. "I haven't decided yet," she responded. "I've not had a chance to give it much thought." Choosing her subject was the furthest thing from her mind, fresh from Jamaica as she was, mango-hued, indecisive. Ersatz consort of Prince Badnigga.

"I expect it will come to you," Liz said cheerfully. "At least I hope for your sake it does, so you don't get stuck and have to pretend to be enthralled by the inventor of the bell sleeve, or the rapes of Zeus, or something." She smiled at Clare and offered her a Player's.

"Why bother if it doesn't interest you?" Clare asked her.

"Because one must," Liz said, simply.

A few days later they met again, by chance, in the stacks,

between the survival of the pagan gods and the Valois tapestries. Liz was taller than Clare, with deep-set blue eyes, magnified by round tortoise-shell eyeglasses, held together at the bridge by a strip of white adhesive. She was quite beautiful but mocked her looks, saying she felt like the offspring of Virginia Woolf and Simone Weil.

The two women whispered in the gray of an afternoon in February. "I'm on my way to my school this evening, an old-girls' weekend . . . care to come along?

"It's quite a pretty drive," Liz added, hesitantly.

"Where is it?"

"Gravesend . . . but don't let the name distress you . . . a town at the mouth of the Thames . . . literally where the graves end . . . anyone passing beyond that point is buried at sea. . . . Sorry, didn't mean to be morbid."

Clare was taken by the guidebook description but also by quick, vivid memories of *Schoolfriends,* the comic book which arrived each month in Jamaica, hanging from a line in the Chinese shops, devoured by the girls at St. Catherine's, and Wolmer's and St. Andrew's and St. Hugh's and even Immaculate Conception. Images of a *real* girls' school were to be found within—tuck shop, midnight feasts, austere headmistress. St. Catherine's had a tuck shop, but it stocked meat patties, mangoes, paradise plums, not the unimaginable foreign delicacies of an English tuck shop at an English girls' school. And their headmistress was a large-bosomed creole, auntie of the equally large-bosomed headgirl.

As Clare remembered this longing, which she had shared with so many of the other girls, as they shared the longing for eventual "true love" described by the romance magazines, and the longing to be truly beautiful, pictured in *Photoplay* and *Modern Screen*—as these memories surged and she felt tenderness for how innocent they all had been, how believing of the world, and wondered, What has become of them?—as she thought these things, Liz was continuing her description, calling her old school "a sort of Christ's Hospital for girls . . . you know . . . Lamb . . . Coleridge . . . the school where the boys are made to wear medieval dress? Well, we had to dress as eighteenth-century maidens, like the wards of some old bachelor . . . they didn't say why. . . . I expect they forgot to change the style and created tradition from oversight. They didn't even change when a third-former got tangled in her hem and fell a full flight of stairs. I remember the headmistress at prayers the next morning—'Now, girls, Betty was not a swan. . . . Still, we must remember her fondly . . . and avoid a scandal.' I never quite understood the juxtaposition of those three things . . . that's a lie; of course I did. Poor Betty. . . ." Liz's voice started to betray her, and she quickly changed tone. "Do come. We'll spend a couple of days at the school; then I'll drive us a bit north and show you the Secret Waters . . . they're quite something."

"When are you leaving?" Clare asked.

"About five. Look, if you want to come, I'll pick you up at your room . . . it will be good for both of us to get away from all these dead people . . . hats or no hats." She laughed.

"Thanks for asking me. I think I'd like to come along."

"Good; until five, then."

"Until five."

Dickensian workhouses, buildings promising chill, clotted porridge, were what met them. Not the ivy-entwined thatched-roof buildings Clare remembered from *Schoolfriends*—close image still, rounded, pastoral. No, these were sharp, spired—here she half-expected to see a plaque to the memory of Helen Burns. She kept the joke to herself, remembering Betty.

Inside, the old-girls were friendly enough, saying, some of them, with the best of intentions, she had no doubt, that they had heard Jamaica was "absolutely super." She took the compliment graciously, making no response, not wanting to know from whom they had heard. They were friendly but obviously eager to get to the business of reunion, of memory, and away from their duty to an outsider. Clare understood, not quite sure why she had been asked in the first place, and spent the next day alone, wandering through the town of Gravesend.

She found herself at the church of St. George and took herself into the churchyard to eat her lunch of digestive biscuits and white grapes, bought from a vendor on the High. Sitting there, hearing the foghorns of the distance at the mouth of the river, she let her mind wander, drawn back to Jamaica, wondering what would be her course, suddenly frightened, dismissing her thoughts. There will be time enough to decide—false comfort, and she knew it, but enough at the moment.

Her eyes took on the task of occupying her mind, and she let them scan the graveyard. Lighting finally on the most conspicuous monument, standing above the others. Striking her. She stood and walked toward it—from a distance her training suspected allegory. Bronze. Female. Single figure. Single feather rising from the braids. Moccasined feet stepping forward, as if to walk off the pedestal on which she was kept. A personification of the New World, dedicated to some poor soul who perished in pursuit of it.

Clare came closer. It was not that at all. No; this was intended to signify one individual and mark her resting place. The letters at the base of the statue told her this. Indicating the statue was a gift from the Colonial Dames of America in 1958, in loving memory of their countrywoman, Pocahontas. Clare walked around the statue, slowly, taking it in. The bronze-woman gave nothing else away. She went into the church and found memorials to the Indian princess. Found two stained-glass windows, one showing her baptism, full-grown, wild, kneeling at the font. Found she had been tamed, renamed Rebecca. Found she had died on a ship leaving the rivermouth and the country, but close enough for England to claim her body. In her twentieth year, the pamphlet on display in the vestibule said. Clare donated five pence and put the pamphlet in her pocket. A fever took her on her return to Virginia: "Friend of the earliest struggling colonists, whom she nobly rescued, protected, and helped." The pamphlet said there had been a son.

Clare stayed in the church—cold. Dim light passing through stained glass. Something was wrong. She had no sense of the woman under the weight of all these monuments. She thought of her, her youth, her color, her strangeness, her unbearable loneliness. Where was she now?

As people gathered for evensong, she left the church and walked back to the school. She told one of the old-girls, for Liz was nowhere to be found, that she had been called back to London and would find her way by train. She thanked the old-girl and gave her regrets.

Some months later. A march of the National Front was passing by the windows of the institute, as a seminar on the Hermetic Tradition progressed. Chants. Shouts. Noise slamming against the glass of the well-appointed, high-ceilinged room. KAFFIRS! NIGGERS! WOGS! PAKIS! GET OUT! A banner—white bedsheet with black paint—went past. KEEP BRITAIN WHITE! The voices rose and invaded the room further, forcing the professor to raise his voice, in anachronistic disdain cursing the "blasted miners." As if this phrase would embrace any public display which inconvenienced him. Some of the students smiled—miners, fascists, what did it matter?—and the professor continued, attempting in his high-pitched ramble to convey the connection of the Hermetic Tradition to Giordano Bruno and question whether it had been overstated, but the outside jargon smashed clear through his words, louder, louder: NIGGERS, CLEAR OUT! And Clare, seated opposite the windows, looking out, imagined glass breaking, flying; but nothing happened.

As if in response, as if there could be a dialogue, a poster appeared the next day on a bulletin board outside the cafeteria in Senate House. WE ARE HERE BECAUSE YOU WERE THERE.

A woman on the queue, fellow student named Vivienne Hogg-Hunter, whom Clare barely knew, muttered toward her, "I say, those nig-nogs are a witty lot." When she was met by silence, she barreled on about an uncle in Uganda who had sewn a man's lip back on, bitten off in a fight, she said, a drunken fight, by the man's own wife. Amusement. Silence still. She described in a louder voice the expulsion of the uncle, doctor, missionary, by Idi Amin, that "great ape." Clare turned to the woman. "Why don't you go fuck yourself," she suggested softly.

"Pardon?"

"You heard what I said."

"You can't be defending the policies of Amin," Hogg-Hunter objected.

Clare made no response. She took her tray to a window seat, where she busied her mind with the myth of Callisto, raped by Jupiter in the form of Diana. Seeking the arcane in Arcady. But her face still burned from the encounter on the queue, and she found herself afraid of crying.

"You look a bit down at the mouth." Liz was standing across from Clare. "Mind?" She asked before sitting.

"No, go ahead."

"Well, I've had warmer greetings."

"Sorry." Clare poked her fork through grayish peas.

"What's wrong?"

As briefly as possible, with a voice as dispassionate as she could make it, Clare related the incident of a few moments before.

"I see," Liz responded, touching Clare's hand briefly. "But I don't know why you even bothered. . . . I mean, the woman is lightweight in the extreme . . . poor devil thinks the *Harmonia Mundi* is a pipe organ, for God's sake." She smiled at Clare. "Why even give the bitch the time of day?"

"I had to say something."

"Why? Why not let it go? Some people will live and die stupid, that's all."

"It—the whole thing. Not just her . . . the march yesterday. . . ."

"What march?" Liz asked.

"The National Front . . . surely you heard it?"

"Oh, you mean that bloody rabble . . . Christ! What a racket . . . I had to move my desk in the library."

"It didn't upset you . . . on another . . . level?"

"What do you mean?"

"I mean, to me it felt . . . dangerous."

"Oh . . . I'm sorry. But you needn't take it personally, you know."

"Why do you say that?"

"I mean, you're hardly the sort they were ranting on about."

"That doesn't make it at all better. . . . Besides, I can never be sure about that . . . and I'm not sure I should want . . . ah, exclusion."

"But you are who you are. . . . Look, Hogg-Hunter's words weren't directed at you. . . . Surely you didn't think they were?"

"Liz, you are missing my point."

"Which is?"

"Which is that I am . . . by blood . . . the sort they, and she, were ranting on about."

"But your blood has thinned, or thickened, or whatever it does when . . . you know what I mean."

"You mean I'm presentable. That I'm somehow lower down the tree, higher up the scale, whatever." Clare was having a hard time keeping the bitterness from her voice.

"I mean, I doubt any of your relatives bite off one another's lips."

"Some of my ancestors were Caribs . . . cannibals," Clare said, hoping to end the conversation then and there, using shock, again.

"That's ancestors. Some of mine wore skins and worshiped fire." Liz spoke in a patient tone, apparently unaware of the cold across the table.

Clare got up. "Look, I have some work to do. I'll see you."

"Perhaps at tea?"

One afternoon, after tracing another of Zeus' rapes under the great eyeball, Clare took a break and found herself standing at the bar of the Ploughman, across Museum Street, a letter from Harry/Harriet in her hand.

I find myself closer to my choice, girlfriend. How about you? Jamaica needs her children—I repeat myself, I know. Manley is doing his best but people are leaving in droves—those who can. The poor, the sufferahs, of course remain. I know you think I nag you too much, but there is terrific distress. And there is no end in sight. Write soon.

Love & kisses, H/H.

A man approached her as she read. "You look as if you have the weight of the world on your shoulders."

6

ORGAN HARVESTER

Standing in the truck, should Clare think of Bobby, now at this remove of space and time, should she ponder him at all, their life together, as she moved away from Accompong into high ruinate, she might conjure him as she had conjured him before. Envisioning the detail which caught her as he sat in the pub across from her, resting his left leg on an empty chair.

The wound he carried on his ankle. The place where brown skin split and yellowness dripped from a bright pink gap—no matter what she did. Soon she had taken it upon herself to do something.

Together they left London. She quit the institute as suddenly as she had entered it. Not a momentous decision, she told herself, not a-tall, a-tall; in fact the place fell away from her easily—perhaps too easily, perhaps not. She wrote Harry/Harriet about it, telling her friend a return to Jamaica seemed more and more likely, but she needed time; she asked Harry/Harriet to relay a message to her aunt and uncle: She was fine, but very occupied with school.

Would there come a time in her life, she asked her friend—half serious—when taking leave would not seem the likely conclusion to her every move?

Clare applied herself to the wound. All along their journey she bought patent medicines from each nationality of apothecary they encountered; got ointments and tinctures from homeopathic pharmacists in whatever town she and Bobby tossed up—shops on cobbled streets behind windows filled with indigo, cobalt, aquamarine liquids held in glass jars labeled in gilt, ginseng root climbing a corner of the pane, transparent envelopes of comfrey, rue, jupiter's-beard scattered about. An old man in an alpine village, starting almost imperceptibly as he glimpsed Bobby outside the shop, offered Clare a packet of pale powder, the dried flesh of a sea urchin, he said, most effective, an ancient curative, but its guarantee could not be extended to certain types of skin—he shrugged. In Arles, a practitioner sold her yarrow, *Achillea millefolium,* used by Achilles to heal his men—a warrior's poultice. A middle-aged woman interrupted him, shaking her head, and saying No, he spoke nonsense. She spoke with the authority of a witch, telling Clare salt was the thing, famous for its property of drawing infection. Acrid, sweet, stinging, soothing—none of these were of help. The wound still dripped.

She held compresses against Bobby's skin—these she fashioned from gauze she soaked overnight in the sink of their hotel room, in still mineral water and heavy brown soap—to no effect. She bought an aloe plant in a florist's shop in Turin and split a leaf then and there in the middle of the majolica-tiled room—the tiles illustrating the metamorphoses of Hyacinthus and Narcissus; at once Ovid came back at her—squeezing the thick juice into her friend's gaping skin: *locus,* theme of visual representation fitting the place of decoration, passed through her head, as Bobby sat on a bench of wrought iron, his boonie cap hiding his eyes. He went along with her ministrations, assuming they were for her as much as him, telling her gently she might as well use her medicines to make rain.

She was afraid he was right. The aloe vera had been a last resort, dredged from a memory of her grandmother, so far from her then, and even that had not worked.

The wound was livid and refused to heal. Not even when she elevated his bare foot in her lap hour upon hour while Bobby slept beside her on a train crossing the Sierra de Guadarrama, passing the Escorial, descending into the Valle de los Caídos. His ankle might stop throbbing for a while, the lips of the wound move closer together almost to join, but the least jolt and it would open again and the flow of pus would begin.

Drawn to him as friend; later, lover. But also as protector and healer. She felt her petty, private misery recede, faced with the concreteness of his broken skin. Still—she failed him. She could not stop the flow of pus, she could not prevent the cold eyes against his brown skin.

"Girlfriend, I am glad you have found somebody," Harry/Harriet wrote her at the American Express office in Barcelona.

> I hope he is good to you, and you to him. Please keep in touch and let me know how it goes. Looks like your uncle and auntie to move to Miami. Mi dear, mi dear, the rats are truly deserting the ship—the rats' nests stand empty, and the mahogany and china gather dust. No offense meant, present company included, and all that. I understand your need for time. Frederick and Violet say your grandmother place is left to you now. Their new address is enclosed, for they may not get the chance to write before they grab their cash and lif' up.
>
> Love & kisses,
> H/H.

P.S. I am so pleased you have left the motherland. I like to think of you in prettier places.

P.P.S. Have you ever read C.L.R. James? One impressive bredda dat. I am in the middle of *The Black Jacobins*—I tell you, girlfriend, the history they didn't teach us . . . nuh mus' 'fraid? I think I have fallen in love—with Jean Jacques Dessalines. (Smile)

Bobby's explanations to her about the reason for his wound varied. He said he could not remember what had caused it. And, man, it was an awful long time ago. Dream-like, he said. Like an event in a dream that on waking seems at once certain and complete, he would recollect a cause, only to have it disappear, change absolutely, immediately, as his mind convinced him that this made no sense—it hadn't been like that. Man, haven't you ever had something happen to you that you can't bring back? He told her it was like trying to reconstruct a landscape after a lightning flash when you have never seen the landscape before. Often, he said, the entire thirteen months he spent over there felt like that. The landscape shot with flashes of light—harsh, rapid. A violent nakedness ensuing. Bobby seemed to believe in each explanation without question, only to reject it when another occurred to him.

A sharp bare branch grazed him as he traveled silently from a silver airplane through blur sky into a spectral tree. He cast the terrain for her. She couldn't picture it. A country with burns across its surface. Not like a desert, no, not at all, he said, a thick green landscape stripped by the chemical held in a striped drum, which he had worn in a tank strapped to his back, so he told her. She couldn't envision it, not clearly, but she did remember the bleeding landscape near Fern Gully, rusted, orange, where the ore had been scraped from the country. Emerging from the dark of the green cave, arched by primeval growth, emerging from the brake to find machines at work stripping the bauxite from the country. She and Harry/Harriet had been on their way to the bottomless Blue Hole.

At other times, Bobby told her a pongi stick tipped with an arcane poison was to blame. Sometimes a broken

146

beer bottle, on the littered ground of a Soul City. A thin-bladed knife flying at him in a scuffle. A piece of rusted wire from a detonated booby trap hiding in the tall grass. A sun-dried shinbone, slivered by shrapnel. The jawbone of a wa-ter buffalo—he told her he had been playing Samson. He smiled.

He smiled. Did it really matter, he asked her, when his imagination had given up; did it matter that much, all that much, to know how the wound was made? Wasn't the only important thing that it would always be his—something he must learn to live with?

She had not until now known anyone who had gone to war, she told him. There had been a boy in her neighbor-hood written up in the paper. An Italian American, first-generation college, only son, basketball player at St. John's, who had joined up, who had walked forward onto an Amer-ican land mine. He died. A folded flag and medal returned. His mother jumped from the roof of the office building she cleaned. When the police opened the woman's apartment, the *News* reported, and found a dollar sign painted in bright-red enamel on the wall behind an altar to her son—photo-graph of him in marine dress, candle to Our Lady, rosary, plastic yellow roses—they concluded she was crazy. Bobby nodded. But, Clare said, she had not known the boy person-ally at all, only from a distance.

Once, sitting in an outside bar of a Yugoslavian work-ers' resort called Blue Lagoon, open to foreigners, the black ribbon of a sand viper had run across her foot. Otis Redding was on the sound system and a bottle of slivovitz on the table. When she had drunk so much slivovitz that she couldn't feel her top lip when she spoke, she asked him to tell her more. What did you actually do? Why do you want to know? he questioned her, meeting her green eyes with his brown ones. I care for you; I need to know.

He smiled at her and told her he was an organ har-vester. He danced, he said. Danced through the war. Danced through the aftermath of firefights, gathering bits and pieces dancing with a life all their own, carrying them back to the doctors, gaily dancing all the while—hear me, Bojangles— and the bag which contained the remains also danced—an electricity of motion—rhythm, man. An organ harvester tripping through a rice paddy, up to his knees in warm water, running a homemade wooden rake, like his mother had used to glean shrimp from the river, under the scummy surface, tinted pink, to catch hold of the hearts and lungs and livers. And the minds. Lord Jesus, yes. That hugely beautiful organ. Infinity of potential. Soul. Shit. He laughed further— she wanted him to stop but couldn't tell him, she had asked for this—he laughed further and told her the doctors had been on the verge of knowing how to encase one man's brain in another man's skull—to see how his vision might change . . . to eliminate waste. You see, baby, I was a life-giver. He stopped suddenly and sang along with Otis. *Wasting time.*

It was in his sleep, in his nightmare, that he harvested organs. Standing at the edge of a lush field, he entered the frame of his dream, dragging a green Glad bag behind him. He was alone at first. He had certainty. He knew absolutely why he was there. To glean American organs from underneath the surface of the cloudy water. In the dream he began slowly, and then began to speed, throwing hearts and lungs and livers into the bag in no particular order, having trouble keeping up, only briefly checking to see whether they were stamped DMZ. Speeding up. That was imperative. He had a quota. Urgent. He didn't have time to sort through all the pieces. He barely had time to clean the teeth of his rake. Scraps of mind, trapped by their convolutions, hung from the wooden pegs.

"Why will you rape me?" Her English was precise. He did not respond. "You cannot rape me. You are Black."

She said nothing else.

A white sergeant was suddenly there. Standing over them, his head encased, surrounded by a helmet of stained glass. He jammed a fat piece of heart into her mouth. His eyes were masked by the flash glass.

The sunlight passing through the helmet played across Bobby and the woman, illumined them. Now yellow . . . blue . . . red. Flashing across the face of the woman on the ground and the body of the man kneeling beside her. The colors made them beautiful.

They were going to kill her anyway.

He woke and sat up in the white-sheeted, white-barred bed. Desperate to imagine other things.

He put his head back into the pillow wet from his sweat and shut his eyes. No good. He saw her again. Her eyes leaking water at the sides. Shut. Waiting. She was tiny like so many of them. And ageless. She could have been fifteen. She could have been fifty.

There was a group of soldiers standing around, their eyes covered by masks of steel, wings on either side. He saw himself—still kneeling. He knew he had to live with these men. He had to walk in front of them, while their steel wings carried them on air.

She would be dead but he would be alive. But before he could get his penis free of his pants they shot her. Her brain flew sideways from her skull. Her teeth clamped the piece of choice heart tight.

The helmeted sergeant, eyeless—the colors of his head interrupted by soft lines of lead—spoke. "You didn't think I'd let you fuck her alive, did you, boy?"

Bobby did not answer. He woke again and sat up. Soaked. Tangled in the blankets and the sheets. He must have turned a thousand times. A thousand minutes must have gone by. He looked at the alarm and found it five minutes past his last awakening. The room was dark but he could make out some of the sleeping men around him. Interrupted men. Some with tubes in them. Some with pulleys holding their limbs free of their bodies. Some with intravenous contraptions hooked into their veins. Some with flat sheet in unexpected places.

Again he put his head down, straightened the bed as best he could, and shut his eyes.

There was a brightness behind his eyelids. The terrain was waiting.

Again the sergeant ordered him. He couldn't do it. He started to cry. His penis began to drip and he peed on the woman in the black pajamas. He felt an incredible terror. He couldn't feel anything else.

Whitemen watched him as he peed and wept. Still kneeling, unable to get up. He peed like he peed in his pants when he was five and some whitemen scared him in the wrong toilet—he could not yet read. The men in the dream smiled, then turned and dragged their iron-clad eyes back out of the frame. He was left with the dead woman.

He woke again, determined to stay awake. If he shut his eyes the whole thing would start all over. His catheter had pulled free and the warmth of fresh piss began to spread. To become suddenly cold.

After he left the hospital and the army declared him cured, he was given two choices for further duty, both in his home state, Alabama. Riot control or funeral detail—he chose the latter.

For several months he wandered the backroads with a white officer missing a leg, telling poor people their sons were dead, having died of course as men. The fathers, were there fathers, kept their silence. The mothers pounded the chests of the messengers. After one particularly furious mother knocked the lieutenant off balance, kicking red dirt against his remaining five inches of right leg, as he lay in the country dust, a sorrowful sweat gathering in the creases of his face—after this, Bobby became the sole news-giver, the lieutenant grateful to be but an exhibit.

The entire time the dream was with Bobby. The army shipped him to Stuttgart in 1969. He asked to speak with a Black chaplain; he was shown to a white psychiatrist. A man who was all seriousness and indecision, and in his confusion jumped on what he thought was the obvious: Bobby's difficulty with whites as authority figures and envy of their power—"love-hate relationship" fell from the colonel's lips.

Soon after this, but not solely because of it, needing to leave something behind, Bobby walked off the base with papers certifying his discharge, signed General Crispus Attucks—no one was the wiser. He wandered several years—Sweden, Denmark, then London.

Bobby was tired. Inside and out.

"Look," he said to her, after he and Otis had finished, his eyes off somewhere else, tossing back a shot of slivovitz before he went on. "Look, baby . . . this is the thing . . . how to put it—ah, succinctly. . . ." He stretched the last word almost to obscenity. "I have lived with this war for a very long time . . . too long . . . too fucking long. . . . There are things about that time . . . place . . . I need to put behind me . . . bury . . . forget." His voice started out angry but slid gradually to quiet. "There are things I cannot explain . . . things you have no right—that's right—no right to know . . . to ask. My war cannot serve your purpose, whatever that might be.

"Look, do you think we could have a moratorium on the war—whether it be in the form of my foot, nightmares, sweats? Okay?" Before she could answer, he added, almost as a challenge, "I wonder . . . I wonder if you would have come along with me . . . if you'd care . . . want to know me . . . if it had been Jamaica. It could easily have been Jamaica, you know . . . if Fidel had been Ho, for example. That would have given the big daddies a whole lot of other colored people to liberate."

"I couldn't say, Bobby. I'm sorry." She felt rebuked, naïve. Her country was a sandbox, a stage set, Harry/Harriet had said—not a war zone.

"Don't be sorry . . . just say yes. Agree to bury your curiosity. All right?"

"Yes. All right. I promise. Whatever you want. If that's what you want."

She remembered, as she spoke, her father's dictum, oft

repeated when she had asked the circumstances of her mother's departure, "Don't ask about things which don't concern you."

"I can agree, I can be agreeable, in five languages, you know." Her voice became cold. "I was raised by my father to be that way. To be the soft-spoken little sambo, creole, invisible neger, what have you, blending into the majority with ease." She had a sense he didn't trust her in her skin, somewhere he didn't believe she was what she said she was— why should he? "You know, there are people who look one way and think another, feel another. We can be very dangerous, to ourselves, to others. Got to quell one side, honey, so I was taught. Amazing . . . amazing how the other side persists. . . . I can also say 'shit' in five languages . . . perhaps that's my mother's influence. Like my persistence in drifting to the wrong side, what my father would consider the wrong side, what most of my family would consider the wrong side. Who knows? As time passes my mother becomes harder and harder to bring back—but I know . . . I feel she would approve of my . . . the way my sentiments seem to lie." The sounds of James Brown started in the background. *I feel good. I knew that I would.* The jukebox stopped in Motown 1969—Bobby said it made him feel at home.

"You ever go to her grave when you back home?"

"No."

"How come?"

"I didn't want to ask . . . I didn't want to ask . . . I didn't want to upset her people."

"Baby, you afflicted with something rare."

"Not so rare . . . not where I come from."

"They not your people too? Her homeland, your homeland . . . her God, your God?"

"It's more complicated. . . . God forbid I should raise my mother's death with them—her brother and his wife. I would only hear it was my father's fault and, by extension, mine."

"And what if you said to them, Hey, man, woman, you full of shit—in whatever language they would understand— you people are full of shit, my father didn't kill nobody?"

Clare laughed. "Honey, I just don't know. I might be told to leave, that even as old as I am now, I have no place in being rude to my elders—prime taboo, of course, in a system consisting of almost nothing but taboos." She surprised herself with her bitterness. "I might be reassessed in their eyes, my character traced, and it be concluded that I am my father's daughter after all. I might be cautioned for speaking bad in front of the servants, and with all my education setting a dangerous example."

"The servants being Black, of course."

"Of course." She was embarrassed, and tried to make light of this fact. "Of course . . . that's one of the charming things about Jamaica; everyone is Black, it's just that some are blacker than others. . . . It's a question of degree . . . from ace of spades to white cockroach. . . . But you asked about my mother."

"Tell me."

"I think my basic problem . . . difficulty . . . with . . . I do think my father is accountable . . . if we had not left she might well be alive . . . if he had listened to her fears . . . heeded her . . . we might have returned . . . to where we belonged. Home would not be something in my head."

"But he had his dreams too."

"Yes, but how far . . . far from hers they seemed."

"Baby, you got to get to the place where you are apart from your mother, your father, while still being a part of them. For they made you, like it or not. At least, that's how I feel."

"You are lucky, Bobby. So lucky . . . to be one and not both."

"Yeah," he responded; his voice was dry.

Clare drained the last of the slivovitz. The bar was closed; moonlight illumined them as they spoke. The dark jukebox had long since stopped singing.

Bobby stroked her face gently. "You can say more."

"Thanks." She smiled at him, paused. "You know . . . I don't remember if she ever told me she loved me. And if she loved me how could she have left me? I know that sounds childish." She was suddenly self-conscious, apologetic.

"Maybe she did; maybe she didn't. Maybe she figured not telling you would make you strong. Maybe she was the kind of woman love didn't come easy to. Maybe she didn't have much of it in her life, and so it was hard for her to pass it on."

"Like me?"

"What do you mean?"

"I mean . . . love. . . ." The word at once sounded wholly ridiculous—and she with it. She wanted nothing more than to splash cold water on her face, which was burning. "Forget it . . . just forget it."

"No; tell me."

"All right. I mean *it*, love, affection, does not come easy to me—"

"Maybe not to any one of us." He interrupted her.

"Either the giving or the receiving." It was as if she had not heard him. "I do not trust it . . . myself with it. I am not even sure what it means. I feel like a shadow . . . like a ghost . . . like I could float through my days without ever touching . . . anyone. I truly cannot remember when I did not feel this way. Locked off. I could have lived and died under that goddamned eyeball tracing things not meant to concern me."

"I don't think so . . . then you wouldn't have come with me. You are not attached yet. They have yet to claim you. . . . Can you love yourself?"

". . . I don't trust myself with feeling." The only response she could bring herself to make.

"We all have that trouble, baby."

"Sometimes I think I feel for you only because you're wounded. . . . Sorry, I am not being agreeable. I promised I wouldn't mention that again. Sorry."

Bobby ignored her lapse. "You mean actually wounded, with a ten-year-old hole in my foot, or . . . or because I'm a Black man?"

"I mean you're not foreign to me." She evaded him.

"What exactly do you mean?"

"That we seem to understand each other . . . for some reason."

"We have begun to understand each other, yes."

They were quiet after that, facing a cove in the Adriatic, as the sun began its climb over the water. They walked toward the sloping rockface that separated them from the sea. Descended, sending bits of rock, perhaps shards of pots, for this was a place of ruins, sliding below them, bouncing and flying, as they themselves gained speed. They reached the sea, slipped from their clothes, and let the waters cover them.

He entered her, coming into her along with the salt sea. Her own liquid rushed out, and they stood, bodies wrapped, one with the water.

Feeling only a tiny shot of guilt, Clare wrote to her aunt and uncle in Miami, telling them she was doing work for her degree on the continent, describing briefly the beauty of churches, managing to get more money from them in the process, as well as a letter extolling the tranquility of the mainland after the turbulence of the island, caught as it was in riot, fire, burn. "My dear, you wouldn't recognize the place," her uncle closed.

When the money came, Bobby and Clare took off again.

Paris. Things started to happen fast. The war returned with a vengeance on the both of them. This was the beginning of the end. So it felt.

The dark interior of Notre Dame. She knelt before the statue of St. Joan in the back of the sanctuary. Lighting a candle to the saint. Remembering the blue pin she wore on her uniform when she belonged to the house of Arc. *I will dare, and dare, and dare, until I die.* The manly girl, the roaring girl might mock her now. Please, St. Joan, make it not be true, she prayed childishly. More wish than prayer—is when you going to realize you woman, girl? If it is true then it is true. To whom had Pocahontas prayed?

When she returned to the hotel she told Bobby her fear and he was forced then and there to reopen the war. Wearily telling her about the chemical he had sprayed on the terrain. Yes, baby, that was the true story. Not organ harvesting, no. No, that was the joke. But you knew that already. No, honey, the reason my foot can't heal—it don't matter one bit how the hole was made—the reason it can't heal, the secret of its stubbornness, can be found in a drum with an orange stripe. I learned all about it when I hooked up with some bloods in Copenhagen . . . deserters like me. All not quite right . . . physically, I mean. Yes, baby girl, I'm a deserter. I didn't tell you that before. I didn't know if I trusted you. If I could trust you. Can I trust you? (He did not wait for her to answer.) Anyway the bloods filled me in . . . about aftereffects. From walking, spraying, dusting forests, paddies, all of that, as far as the eye could see, people's farms, homes, villes, filling my canteen from streams seasoned with it, drinking it in, washing my body with it. We should have known.

Ever see the movie *The Incredible Shrinking Man?* Where the dude gets covered by that fine mist? (She nodded.) Think of that. It entered me. It doesn't end with me. So if what you think might be true turns out to be true, you better think abortion, honey. Unless you want a little Black baby with no eyes, no mouth, no nose, half a brain, harelip, missing privates, or a double set like some fucking hyena, missing limbs, or limbs twisted beyond anything you might recognize, organs where they are not meant to be, a dis-harmony of parts—any or all of the above, or the above in combination, better think again, sweetness. (As he spoke, a confusion of emotion was in her—and she wondered at the coldness in his voice.)

Look, I will stay with you, he offered. I have a few hash johnnycakes left, and we still have some of your uncle's money if what I get isn't enough. I know my responsibility, I ain't trying to slide from under it. Not my style. Not to worry. It will be over soon. I will stay with you. I saw one of these babies—a messed-up little thing, scarred over where doctors tried to clean up the mess. Do you understand why I sound so cold? I don't think you need my nightmare made flesh, that's all. Some little wood's colt turned to monster. Heavy . . . heavy. (He laughed at himself, a scratch of a laugh.)

She only felt empty. Turning from him, looking out the sooted window to the street, she focused her eyes on the Gitanes sign below, watched the shopkeeper as he locked up, trying not to think. There had been a certain thrill in her uncertainty—she could admit this now—and that was gone. The gypsy on the sign dimmed and went out. Other shops were shutting, and she fancied the homecomings of the shopkeepers.

When the street was closed for the night she turned back to Bobby and sat next to him on the bed. "I'm sorry," she said.

"We should have known," he said again.

In the end she was removed from decision. Another reprieve from womanhood? Answered prayers? She could not tell. Something slid out of her suddenly—it could have been a late, heavy period for all she knew, or a baby with half a brain. Relief. Reddening the sheets they were twisted in. Thickly red. It was startling to see Bobby streaked in her blood. He woke to it, swore softly, and walked into the shower. He said nothing directly to her, nor she to him. She soaked the bedclothes in the sink, so the concierge would be no wiser and embarrass her by a comment—her father's daughter emerged at odd times. The girl taught to conceal unsettling evidence of herself. God forbid that some fucking woman who overcharged them for the room, who whispered something to her dog each time they entered or left,

157

whom Clare would never see again once she quit this place—God forbid this woman should know Clare bled. She resisted a desire almost overwhelming to examine the clots of blood, floating free of the sheet, running down the drain. How primitive, my girl, she mocked herself. The last stains lifted with salt, seeming to diminish before her eyes. What had happened was behind her. Not so.

Bobby's nightmares, once confined to sleep, were let loose. Engaging his mind when he was awake. He had tried to protect her from them before this—the depth of them. The war slid in whenever his effort to will it away let down. Incessant. He took extraordinary means to stay it. Sometimes reciting the words to every poem he could dredge, things he had spoken in a backwoods school when he was a boy. The poems ran together into nonsense. He began to scream. To rock himself back and forth, slowly, then speeding, violently, as if his head would roll from his shoulders.

"Try to think of other things," she asked him. "Please. . . . Think of the times when you were a boy . . . the things you told me about fishing with your grandmother, catching shrimp with your mother . . . gathering okra, and dodging the snakes . . . try to think of other things."

"There are no other things—not now. Don't you understand, girl?"

He sang hymns. The tunes of the Assembly of God, long gone.

"Bobby, I'll stay with you. I'm not going to leave you."

He stared at her. "Why not? You'd be crazy if you didn't."

She held him. He screamed. He saw something which was not her. "Don't leave me with him . . . please . . . please don't leave me with him!"

"With who, Bobby? With who?"

He seemed to forget what he had said. "I don't know," he answered, curling his body away from her.

He refused to eat, saying all food came from a drum with an orange stripe. It was too late, he told her. They were all tainted. Touched.

"You have her face! Why are you doing this to me?"

"I am Clare. Nobody else. I am here with you. We are in Paris. The war has been over long time now. . . ." This had become her litany, spoken so often as to be meaningless. "Please. Please, let me get you something to eat."

"Okay," he said suddenly, looking at her with eyes exhausted from his sadness. "Okay. Okay. I'll eat something. . . . Can I trust you?"

"Yes, you can trust me. I am Clare. I love you."

She left him at the hotel that afternoon; as she turned back to look at him he was sitting in a corner, staring somewhere beyond the room, not reacting to her promise to return soon. He seemed at that instant peaceful. She hoped. She hoped he would not scream and draw fire when she was not there to protect him. She had greased the palm of the concierge so many times by now, the woman could probably make a down payment on the Palais du Papes, Clare thought to herself, forcing a smile as she passed the desk, the woman, and her wretched little dog. "Madame." She spoke in greeting. The woman nodded.

She walked down St. Michel, across the Pont Neuf, through the gardens of the Louvre, ending her journey at American Express, L'Opéra, finding, to her joy, amid the blue-jeaned hordes and pasteled and leisured groups, cursing these apparently contented people, a letter from Harry/Harriet.

Yes, she told herself, she had promised to return to the hotel soon, and would rush back with food, but she needed this letter, this company, needed a relief from that room, and her feelings that she had brought all this on.

She took herself back in the direction of the river and sat in a café in the Tuileries, where she drank a glass of red wine.

*

Darling girlfriend,

I write you this letter on a day of national mourning. We have descended as low as we can go. Let me tell you what happen. Today we are supposed to be remembering the grandmothers of our people. We are supposed to be remembering, through our hypocrisy, the 167 old women who burned up in a fire started by some bastard. It has something to do with politics, the *Gleaner* say. One side wish to bring shame 'pon the other so them set fire to some old women. Is what kind of world this, girlfriend? Is how long we must endure? We are in a fury down here. If you could have heard their screams, girlfriend. If you could have seen the faces of the few who survived. If you could have heard our rassclat leaders scatter blame. That is the news from home.

How are you? You going to marry your man? When you come back here I have much to tell you. I have been making changes in my life, darling. We got to do something besides pray for the souls of our old women.

Love & Kisses,
H/H.

When Clare returned to the hotel, the concierge stopped her. Saying something about the bill being due.

7

MAGNANIMOUS
WARRIOR!

Magnanimous Warrior! She in whom the spirits come quick and hard. Hunting mother. She who forages. Who knows the ground. Where the hills of fufu are concealed. Mother who brews the most beautiful tea from the ugliest bush. Warrior who sheds her skin like a snake and travels into the darkness a fireball. Mother who catches the eidon and sees them to their rest. Warrior who labors in the spirit. She who plants gunga on the graves of the restless. Mother who carves the power-stone, center of the world. Warrior who places the blood-cloth on the back of the whipped slave. She who turns her attention to the evildoer. Mother who binds the female drumhead with parchment from a goat. Warrior who gathers grave-dirt in her pocket. Pieces of chalk. Packs of cards. Bits of looking-glass. Beaks. Feet. Bones of patoo. Teeth of dogs and alligators. Glass eyes. Sulfur. Camphor. Myrrh. Asafoetida. Frankincense. Curious shells. China dolls. Wooden images. She writes in her own blood across the drumhead. Obeah-woman. Myal-woman. She can cure. She can kill. She can give jobs. She is foy-eyed. The bearer of second sight. Mother who goes forth emitting flames from her eyes. Nose. Mouth. Ears. Vulva. Anus. She bites the evildoers that they become full of sores. She treats cholera with bitterbush. She burns the canefields. She is River Mother. Sky Mother. Old Hige. The Moon. Old Suck.

Rambling mother. Mother who trumps and wheels counterclockwise around the power-stone, the center of the world. Into whose cauldron the Red Coats vanished.

What has become of this warrior? Now that we need her more than ever. She has been burned up in an alms-house fire in Kingston. She has starved to death. She wanders the roads of the country with swollen feet. She has cancer. Her children have left her. Her powers are known no longer. They are called by other names. She is not re-spected. She lies on an iron bedstead in a shack in Trench Town. She begs outside a rumshop in Spanish Town. She cleans the yard of a woman younger than she. She lies in a bed in a public hospital with sores across her buttocks. No one swabs her wounds. Flies gather. No one turns her in the bed. The pain makes her light-headed. They tell her she is senile. They have taken away her bag of magic. Her teeth. Her goat's horn. We have forgotten her. Now that we need her more than ever. The nurses ignore her. The doctors make game of her. The priest tries to take her soul.

Can you remember how to love her?

8

HOMEBOUND

one moment old lady
more questions
what happened to the ocean in your leap
the boatswain, did he scan
the passage's terrible wet face
the navigator, did he blink or steer the ship
through your screaming night
the captain, did he lash two slaves to the rigging?
for example?
lady, my things
water leaden
my maps, my compass
after all, what is the political
position of stars?

    —DIONNE BRAND, "CANTO II," *Primitive*
    Offensive

She left Paris. After a week of waiting around to see if Bobby would come back. Looking for him in the streets. Bars. Around the monuments. Checking the Vietnamese restaurants along rue Monsieur le Prince—self-consciously describing the slender Black man in camouflage who was, she spoke softly, *un blessé de guerre*—thinking this description foolishly romantic, while knowing it true. She was frightened for him, of the harshness of reaction should he begin a rant. But she could wait no longer. And what would she be waiting for? No. She paid the concierge to store the things he left behind and took her leave. Gathering her own possessions, selling some books, and booking passage on a boat to Kingston, embarking at Le Havre, with a stop at Southampton.

One last look at the mother-country, the coast and cliffs which had been drummed into her at St. Catherine's. She took notice, then turned away. She kept to herself on the voyage.

*

"How you feelin', girlfriend?" Harry/Harriet appeared through several levels of consciousness in a room in Kingston Hospital with louvers turned down against the sun. Dark specks left by flies flecked the yellow walls.

"Harry?"

"Harriet, now, girlfriend . . . finally."

"Then you have it done?"

"No, man. Cyaan afford it. Maybe when de revolution come . . . but the choice is mine, man, is made. Harriet live and Harry be no more."

"What you mean, cyaan afford it? What about family?"

"Well, girlfriend, once I tell them my choice, them nuh cut off mi water? Not literally, mind you. . . . Look like what Hyacinth say about me being there on sufferance is too true . . . too true . . . but of course I know dat all along. Wha' fe do?" Harriet shrugged. "But, you know, darling, castration ain't de main t'ing . . . not a-tall, a-tall." She smiled down at Clare in the bed, ribboned cap signifying she was a registered healer. A yellow doctress. "Can get you something?"

Clare thought to say "more morphine" but knew her last dose had not been that long ago—and knew too well what a principled creature Harriet was. The drug did more than stem the pain; she slipped into its arms and was held. She thought of her sister's punctured arms; no wonder.

Clare shook her head. "No thanks, my friend."

Harriet tucked in the sheets as Clare drifted off, kissing her lightly on the forehead. "I was worried for you."

Clare had suffered what Harriet delicately called "women's troubles," common kitchen term from her boyhood. She had arrived in Kingston with a high fever, in pain, entering the city on the sea as her ancestors had once done. Some concealed below. Some pacing above, bonnets protecting their finely complected faces from the brutal sun. Windward Passage. Spanish Main. Contrary images. The noises of the kin below breaking the breezes of the tropical night. Crux bright above them, dark nebula invisible within. Lying on the polished deck while men from Goa cleaned around her, she drifted in and out, thinking, If Jamaica has nothing else, she has at least her beauty. Sun lighting the whiteness of the cays, corals, reefs. Wreck. Drunkenman. Galleon. Old. Manatee. Gallows. Blue Mountains startling in the distance as the ship passed into the perfect harbor, dolphins in its wake, passing Port Royal, wickedest place in Christendom, once. Perfect. Wickedest. Jamaica had her absolutes. Now, into dream, a deep quake shook her, the earth split under the sea. The city was burning, the sea began to boil. Bobby was wandering through this mess of a dream dragging his foot. What had become of him? She woke. Chilled, under a hot sun. Leaving Bobby, she remembered her mother telling her how Port Royal sank, the pirates, the slave-traders, brethren of the coast, punished by God for their wickedness. The dead, her mother told her, even the dead had been upended, flung into space from their graves, so that no one could tell how many had been killed by the quake and how many had been resurrected. Her mother had laughed at that. Suddenly she could recall her mother's laughter. Then it was gone.

Through her haze she saw men drawing in their nets at Gunboat Beach. Turning, the ship moved closer its berth, near the Esso refinery on Marcus Garvey Drive.

A raging infection in her womb, the doctor finally told her. She had carried it for some time—several weeks at least, he said. Are you promiscuous, my girl? You are probably sterile, he continued, not waiting a response. We can't say absolutely. But that is the usual result.

She took this in. All that effort for naught. Lightening up. Eyes for naught. Skin for naught. Fine nose for naught. Mule—most likely. Circling the cane-crusher.

Clare felt emotion edging in and was afraid she could not stay it. Telling herself it was probably withdrawal from the morphine they had cruelly stopped the day before made no difference—she was dangerously close to giving in, in front of this stranger, coolly intimate with her private parts, her future as a woman.

Harriet had found her last evening, sobbing in an undefined remorse, and held her, telling her this was natural—but the sorrow Clare felt was deep, uncontrollable, and she was afraid it would return here and now with renewed power.

A witch-moth slept in a corner of the room, against the ceiling above the doctor's head. Clare concentrated on the moth, drawing herself to it—huge, quiet, black—a being her people called a bat. Short-lived—how long was it? She could not remember. With life so short, why should she sleep it away, on high in that hot room? Why not swoop, wildly, her wingspan glancing at the doctor's straightened hair, knocking his glasses askew? Then Clare remembered the delicacy of moths, their wings as fine and flimsy as a bougainvillea. She thought of touching her, the grain of her pattern black on black.

"Look at me, girl," the doctor commanded her from her imaginings. "Is what in the ceiling you find so fascinating?"

She focused her eyes on his face but said nothing.

"Don't you understand what I am telling you?"

"I understand," she responded, and turned her eyes back to the moth, wondering what would make her stir.

"So what happened to your soldier man, girlfriend?"

"He's gone. It's a long story."

"Tell me."

"He told me something which cost him too much . . . something he didn't want to tell me . . . something, in the end, he didn't need to tell me."

"Him have wife?"

"If only it had been that simple . . . no . . . someday I'll tell you; not now. I need to put it behind me. I'm too tired. And it's too close."

"You angry?"

"Not angry. Tired."

"I'll leave you to your rest."

*

Once her working hours at the hospital were finished, Harriet traveled through the yards of downtown, in her uniform and carrying her bag, sometimes wearing a red cape, a dashing figure even in the heat, like Mary Seacole, crossing open drains and bending her height into dark interiors. But this was not Scutari, and these were not the Queen's cavalries. Harriet nursed all manner of illness and wound, turning from none. Brushing through barriers of colored plastic strands, dipping herself, touching here and there. She was a fortunate woman, one who had found her true vocation.

While Clare had been dragging her ass through parts unknown, as Harriet put it, her friend had been studying the healing practices. At the university and with old women in the country, women who knew the properties of roots and leaves and how to apply spells effectively. How to temper dengue fever, to slow TB, to stop gangrene in its tracks. Some of the old women saw their knowledge used at the cancer treatment centers for rich Americans, springing up here and there. One old woman, one who kenned Harriet's history, called her Mawu-Lisa, moon and sun, female-male deity of some of their ancestors.

None of her people downtown let on if they knew a male organ swung gently under her bleached and starched skirt. Or that white powder on her brown face hid a five o'clock shadow. Had they suspected, what would they have been reduced to? For her people, but a very few, did not suffer freaks gladly—unless the freaks became characters, entertainment. Mad, unclean diversions.

Had they known about Harriet, they would have indulged in elaborate name-calling, possibly stoning, in the end harrying her to the harbor—perhaps.

And still she was able to love them. How was that?

It was with Harriet and at her suggestion that Clare went to St. Elizabeth for the first time in twenty years, to find her grandmother's place, now left to her, and visit the river and forest of her girlhood. Harriet said she had to start somewhere. When Clare asked her what she meant, Harriet responded that if she came to country with her, Clare would know soon enough.

The house could not be seen at all. The house so hidden it seemed to exist no longer. Once the center of their life in this place. The structure which held her grandmother's stern church. Her grandfather's senility. Her mother's schoolbooks, wormed, yellow, handed down. The building where it was, where she remembered it as being, screened by green. Nothing but the chaos of the green—reaching across space, time too it seemed. When only Arawaks and iguanas and birds and crocodiles and snakes dwelt here.

Before landfall. Before hardship.

Clare found her way to the river, and they cut through. Through the deep green informed with red and yellow and purple, some growth she did not recognize. The strip of water moving over rocks and gathering into pools—narrower, shallower than she remembered. Rocks still white from washerwomen, worn smooth from the steady water and the slap-slapping of cloth—the gossip, laughter, judgment of half-naked women, skirt hems tucked into underpants' legs, squatting, slapping, feet propped against rock as water cascaded across their brownness.

The importance of this water came back to her. Sweet on an island surrounded by salt. She shut her eyes and let the cool of it wash over her naked body, reaching up into her as she opened her legs. Rebaptism.

Suddenly she smiled—she remembered Miss Naomi, the butcher's wife, who each Saturday dragged huge enamel pans of tripe to the river and dipped and cleaned, and cleaned and dipped, until the intestine was pure-white, and the dung ran through the water and down into the sea. Miss Naomi caught her good one day, beginning her task before Clare had finished bathing in the pool below.

The memory completed itself in her head, and her amusement turned to shame. She saw herself standing, naked, covered in dung, screaming at a dark woman older than her mother, "This is my grandmother's river! You have no right . . . !" To which the woman screamed laughter in response, telling Clare only Massa God could possess river, and she, Miss Naomi, whose mother was a coffee-picker, but a decent woman never mind, had permission from Oshun and the Merry Maids to do her business freely and no facey pickney had no right to give her contention.

Clare felt her face redden, even at this distance. Lifting her head she could see the exact spot where she had stood, could almost see the shade of the arrogant child.

She lay back in the water and shut her eyes again.

Harriet broke into her thoughts. "Tell me about being a little girl here, darlin'."

"What would you like to know?"

"What did you do with yourself?"

Clare lightened her voice. "The usual things, I guess. Played dolls. Made believe. Made believe a lot. From the movies . . . books . . . the 'real' world. Pretended I was Pip in *Great Expectations*—my favorite book. Pretended I was Sidney Carton. Peter Pan. Even Columbus, God help me." She saw her young self differently now—alone, escaped—machete tied to her waist, flag made of Christmas wrap fixed to a strip of bamboo, flourishing the machete and planting the flag, claiming the river—still laying claim to the river, she thought—claiming the river for Isabella, Queen of Spain. Far more mysterious than dowdy old Victoria or tight Elizabeth.

"I explored the country. First with my mother. She felt about this place . . . it was where she was alive, came alive, I think. She knew every bush . . . its danger and its cure. She should have stayed here. In America she was lost . . . the tree with the sweetest mango seemed her cherished goal . . . and she always managed to find it in deep bush." As she spoke, picturing the two of them, the recent past invaded, and she wondered how efficiently the chemical in the striped drum could strip her mother's landscape. "I was fortunate I knew her here." She heard her voice, clipped, distant—suddenly—as if she were describing a third-form teacher who had taught her Linnaean classification. No, she said to

173

herself. I was blessed to have her here. Her passion of place. Her sense of the people. Here is her; leave it at that. But Clare did not speak this out loud; she could not trust her voice.

After their bath, they lay together on the rocks, and Clare let herself drift further. Each bend in the river came back to her. The special rocks where crayfish slept underneath. The deep places you could dive without harm. The pool named for a man who suffered from fits. The pool named for a girl made pregnant by an uncle. The dam made by a man who kept hogs. The five croton trees—dragon's blood—marking off the burial place of slaves, at the side of the river, on a slight rise. Unquiet ground, that—children feared the anger of the spirits, who did not rest, who had not been sung to their new home. Her mother had told her of the slaves. Her people. Yes. And their sometime enthusiasm for death. They ate dirt, Kitty told her, when this life became too much for them. And who could blame the poor souls, she continued, who could blame them indeed.

9

DE WATCHMAN

Ogún cuts, in large or small fragments
He kills the husband on the face of fire
He kills the wife on the hearth
He kills the little people who flee outside
Even with water present in the house,
He washes himself with blood.

—YORUBAN HYMN

Had the young man Christopher known this hymn. Had he received the faith it represented. Had he been an iron-worker like the god. Had he been intimate with this ancient god. The mongering god. Had the young man Christopher suspected the power of Ogún in him. The ambivalence of ironwork. The vengeance of the forge. The cold of the chain. The burning edge of the woman clearing cane.

Was the god not damaged by the passage? Was he not born again?

Christopher wandered through the city that morning as his passion calmed and the rum wore off. The young man ached. With a head that felt a hot knife being drawn through it by his own hand. And the smell of their blood around him, inside of him. Mongrel dogs followed after him as if he were one of them. He was convinced of his evil. That his act came from nowhere but his rhyging soul.

Could he read, he would have seen the event cast in thick black letters across *Star* and *Gleaner*. LEADING FAMILY

SLAIN IN STONY HILL. POLICE SEEK CHRISTMAS KILLER. STONY HILL FAMILY CHOPPED. POLICE SEEK YARDBOY FOR HELP WITH THEIR INQUIRIES. SON SURPRISED KILLER. YARDBOY ESCAPED MASSACRE. IDENTITY OF YARDBOY UNKNOWN. NO DESCRIPTION OF YARDBOY. YARDBOY SUSPECT IN FAMILY'S BRUTAL SLAYING. "HE NEVER SAID· A WORD," NEIGHBOR REMEMBERS YARDBOY. MEMORIAL AT ST. CATHERINE'S FOR SLAIN GIRL. POLICE SUSPECT LOVERS' QUARREL BETWEEN YARDBOY AND MAID LED TO MASSACRE. YARDBOY MAY HAVE BEEN MEMBER OF A CULT, POLICE SAY. YARDBOY STILL AT LARGE. "WHEN WILL THIS END?" PRIEST ASKS AT GRAVESITE. POLICE DISCOURAGED.

Soon enough, the newsprint faded, someone else was chopped, a woman sliced in Barbican, a man shot in the head on his verandah in broad daylight.

Never apprehended, he was left to wander. His girlfriend said nothing to the police—licklemos' it could have been we, she told her mumma. Who knew de bwai was mad? Ya, missis, him come within one mile of dis yard, we set de dog 'pon him.

Christopher slept in Maypen Cemetery until they dug it up to pour foundation for more concrete jungle. Glass cities rose around him. The country fell around him even more. He spent his days and nights getting old on the street, retreating from New Kingston to the shanties, shacks, back-o'-wall parts of town he knew, gray boards cotched against each other. His teeth went. Old women offered him tins of watery coffee. He stared at their generosity. Old men squatted in stained khaki, scratching their balls, chewing on jackass rope, offering the predictions of sufferahs. "Wunna see dat tall building yonda—de one that hold us in him shadow? When de earthquake come and de glass shatter, de backra dem and de touris' dem will drop from de sky like Chrismus fat. Sheraton, rass." Christopher walked on. His clothes turned from khaki to crocus sack. His buttocks were visible through a split in the cloth. At the back of a Chinese shop he sucked sugar from a discarded sweetie wrapper. A man drove him off with a firecracker. His hair snaked. He sat in the shadow of Victoria's statue draining the dregs of a Red Stripe bottle. He leaned on a staff, a length of pipe he found discarded in an alley. Some men in knitted caps saying they knew Bob gave him smoke. Eyes red, exploding. His mouth pulled on the spliff; smoke wreathed him.

People say him favor mad. Him favor prophet. He talked when his eyes spun. Soft. Loud. Time passed. He escaped. I am Neger Jesus. I am Neger Christ. Shadow-catcher. Duppy-conqueror. I am the beginning and the end. The bright and morning star.

He was the watchman of downtown.

As such he became known.

A reggae singer wrote a song about him. About de watchman of downtown, walking up and down. To tell we when de time to bu'n it down. Him call fe bu'n. Bu'n de damn t'ing down. Bu'n all Jamaica downtown. People say him mad, dem say him clown, but de truth will come when we bu'n de fockin' place down.

The song was played in Brixton. Children sang it in the streets.

And then came a night when old women burned. De Watchman promenaded, legend now, song now, recognized by spectators drawn by the light and the heat and the terrible smell. Back and forth he walked in front of the fire, old women falling, alive, aflame, into the street. He howled, ran toward the fire, face lit by the heat. Their wisps of hair, thin dresses burned as wicks in the night. He howled, "Dis not de fiah bawn of mi powah! Dis not de fiah bawn of mi powah!" Poor bredda, him mad. Poor bredda, him better watch him nuh catch.

The police picked him up and then they let him go.

> Ogún promenades, serpent poised about his neck.
> Ogún, King of Ire, lord, great sovereign of iron.
> With stripes about his body,
> Such as one sees only on the skin of the wild doe
> Unless it be Akisale, born of the Gaboon viper,
> Unless it be Akisale, born of the python.

> —YORUBAN HYMN

10

THE GREAT
BEAST

No one black dies a natural death.

—JAMAICAN PROVERB

The sun was sinking. The air was becoming cool. At the side of the river Clare woke from her thoughts of landscape, of Kitty, and turned to Harriet, suggesting they walk to Mas' Chai Chang's shop where the railway tracks met and buy some bullah-cakes and aerated water to wash them down.

"Do you remember the flavor they called 'champagne'?"

"Of course, man. Dem still mek it."

"It was my favorite; especially mixed with condensed milk and poured over ice."

"Sound like you home, girl."

They rose, dressed, and set off on foot toward the clay road Clare knew as a girl. Once she put the ruinate of her grandmother's place behind her, the road lay before Clare as a relief map, each feature—house, gully, ancient orange tree—familiar.

They came first to Miss Maxine's Royal Castle Hair

Emporium—a hand-painted sign announced this, a salon held in the one room of Miss Maxine's wattle home. Miss Maxine's daughter-in-Harlem, Carmen, sent her mother a package of the finest relaxer once a month. When the postmistress—who sorted mail in a room behind Mas' Chai Chang's shop—spied the package, word traveled, women flocked, and the Royal Castle filled and overflowed in no time at all. Miss Maxine's home-brewed relaxer worked just as well, but the women enjoyed the intimate contact with something American, and someone always begged Miss Maxine for the empty jar to keep on her dresser, for hairpins, thread, a small bouquet of daisies.

This afternoon the place was quiet, a few chickens scratched around, a green lizard languidly blew a golden balloon from his throat. Miss Maxine was nowhere to be seen, and Clare, forgetting twenty years had passed, was disappointed.

As they walked the road, Clare described to Harriet the other inhabitants, as she remembered them. There was Miss Sarah, who broke rocks to support her wuthless sons; Miss Hattie and Mas' John, who planted their quarter acre with gunga and citrus and marked the crescent-shaped path to their door with whitewashed rocks; Miss Pandora, who sold watered-down rum from her back window; Miss Thyrza, who had only one breast; Mas' Jefferson, called Almighty Jawbone for his talent of bellowing into the night when his cattle, wife, children strayed; Miss Calpurnia, who taught school before the change sent her off her head; Mas' Harold, who fought for the king in World War I and bragged on it; Mas' Jack, who cut his wife on the Sabbath; Miss Belle, who had once saved a man's marriage by curing his impotence—no one said who the man was, nor how Miss Belle had managed this, just that "flesh did not touch flesh"; Miss Naomi, and her husband the butcher, who trudged the road with scales over one shoulder and a sack of flesh over the other; Brother Peter, a Disciple of Christ, once a member of Garvey's legion; Mas' Clem, who mended the wings of birds and kept sick animals in his yard—all the residences remained, a few people were visible on their porches or in their yards. Clare waved at them automatically as she had been taught, and people waved back, wishing good evening to someone they thought was a stranger—all but one old man, who said, "Evenin', Miss Kitty, long time pass, ma'am." "Yes, indeed, sah," Clare responded, not surprised.

At Mas' Chai Chang's shop, a slate of GOODS WE DO NOT HAVE AT THE MOMENT rested against the cement-block exterior. Sugar led the way. Clare left Harriet waiting for the sunset, sitting on an aged bench where the tracks met. Weeds and flowers sprang from the ties and poked their heads from under the gravel between the rails, once tested by the weight of cane.

Clare entered the shop. Inside she saw the whitened head of a woman she recognized as Miss Cherry, the postmistress, bent over her daily paper. She remembered the pose, left hand to brow, right hand gracefully tracing the lines of type in the *Gleaner*. Collecting mail for her grandmother, on her school vacations those years ago, Clare had often interrupted Miss Cherry as she kept up with events.

The shop looked the same to her—same kerosene lamp lit the dark interior, same shelves stood behind the counter, same wooden abacus hung from a nail by a silk thread. But had the goods been so sparse? Had there been so many gaps?

Before Clare could speak, the woman said, without raising her eyes, "If you here fe de Chinaman, him nuh ya."

"Evenin', Miss Cherry," Clare said tentatively.

"Evenin', missis." Miss Cherry paused, wearily leaving her newspaper to examine the visitor. Recognition sparked behind her eyeglasses. "Is who speak to me?"

Clare identified herself through her female line, as was custom, and Miss Cherry nodded at her; confident, she had expected as much—was not too many fair pickney about, and Miss Mattie people had a certain turn to them.

"And how did you find America, Miss Clare?"

There was a distinct crispness in the woman's voice; Clare hedged. "It's a very big country," she responded, stupidly.

"So dem say . . . so dem say. So de *Gleaner* tell we."

Clare nodded, getting Miss Cherry's message that she was a woman who was well informed.

"You like it?" Miss Cherry asked her.

"Not really."

"Seem to tek long time fe decide."

"I haven't been in America all this time."

"So you say." Miss Cherry shrugged and focused her eyes back to her newspaper. "Dem say you mumma didn't cotton to it a-tall, a-tall."

"No; she didn't."

"Me did see she after she get back." Miss Cherry looked at Clare again.

"Yes?"

"She didn't tell you?"

Clare could not remember and was silent.

"Yes, gal, she come back ya so . . . and she remember we . . . even wid her difficulty . . . and disappointment. Such a sweet woman . . . and one who never forget her origin. . . . Pity you don't return wid she, gal."

"Yes."

"So . . . so den . . . is why come you come now, eh?"

"I wanted to see the old place again."

"You see it?" Miss Cherry's tone turned from crisp to bitter. "You see the despair you people lef' it to?"

"I didn't get to the house."

"Gal, ony rat in residence now . . . only rat. And de bush tek everyt'ing else."

Clare was uncomfortable, anxious to change the subject, and remarked, "But the rest of the places on the road look just as they were."

"Perhaps . . . to smaddy come back from long time. People do dem best, yes. But, gal, dem up against it. We is sorely tried. Sorely. T'ings slip from week to week, day to day. You nuh see de slate outside?"

"Yes; I saw it. I don't remember it from before."

"Well, de Chinaman do him best but times is bad . . . two tablespoon of salt cost ten cent one week, fifty cent de next, dollar de one after dat . . . we cyaan draw we belt no tighter, missis. Cyaan draw we belt no tighter. But you will feel dis soon enough, now you back in Jamaica. . . . Maybe you nuh stay."

Indeed, Miss Cherry spoke the truth about the times. There was new government. One party. And shortages—severe. Petrol at ten dollars a gallon—like salt, on the rise. And the dollar falling fast. People said the IMF might repossess the country. It was a time of more hideaways for the rich—the expansion of the sandbox. "Make it your own," the tourist board told the visitors. Tires burned again at roadblocks. And tourists tipped demonstrators who let them pass, easing their escape. No sugar—much of the time. Little rice. No flour. People could buy necessities only by marrying goods, purchasing flour—were there flour—along with a luxury, a jar of chutney, a box of Cheer. No vaccine. But plenty-plenty polio. Children bent up all over the place. Talawa pain, missis, talawa pain.

Some spoke up.

In ancient time dem call mongoose Pharaoh's Rat. Yes, bredda. Yes, sista. It nuh fit? Is nuh Pharaoh's Rat a lead we people? First we get one call himself Joshua. Now dis one from de other side. Him nuh favor rat? Him nuh favor mongoose? De man nuh talk trash? And give shit? Him slick. Him shrewd. Him white him say. Him plan fe build casino fe cure we national debt, him say. Only, him say, no Jamaican can come in, except, him say, fe serve de guest dem. Him say dat progress, bredda, sista. Him mus' nebba hear 'bout Booker T. and him nonsense. Understand, dred? Is Sun City West him plan. Me say de man is Pharaoh's Rat and him Pharaoh live in one big white house across de water. It nuh time fe us fe light de kerosene? And mek de river run red?

*

187

Walking the streets of downtown one afternoon, Harriet spied some of her people gathered in a yard around a black iron pot, cooking something sweet over an open fire. Thyme was in the air. Seeing her, they invited her in and made her welcome. Offering her, their visiting nurse, the first taste of the contents of the pot.

Chicken? No. Not pig neither. Not cow. Is where we would get beef, missis? Nor sheep. Nuh worry yourself is what, doctress, jus' enjoy it nuh?

It was only after sharing their repast, carrying her dish, flattened tin, to rinse over the standpipe, that Harriet recognized what she had eaten. There, near the standpipe, on the trash pile, was the thick green skin of an iguana. The skull nearby, ridged, ugly—Lord Jesus it was ugly. The bright pink of the mouth in grimace. This ancient monster faced her, was in her. She fought the vomit in her throat and took her leave, promising to be by for rounds in a day or so. "Is the best we can do, doctress," a woman whispered to her.

At home she found Clare, a copy of the *Gleaner* in her hands, announcing in broad headlines the theft of several rare lizards from the zoo at Hope. The zoo, the paper reported, was awaiting a ransom note. "Ha!" Harriet spat. The flesh of the beast caught somewhere between her throat and stomach, threatening to rise. "I tell you, girlfriend," she began. "I tell you. What does it mean when we people have to break into a zoo to steal lizard fe nyam? When we people nyam monster? I know dem scavenge and scrounge long time . . . but man, I see the thing. I eat the thing. This different. Different than dog . . . cat. Better mus' come, dem say. No, missis, better never come. We locked past that. We locked in time, sister. We in fockin' lockstep. We ancestor nyam lizard too. And rat. Mongoose, if dem can catch him. Despair too close sometime. Everyt'ing mus' change, sister. Everyt'ing, everyt'ing mus' change." She took a breath. Wiped her face with a hankie. The thing she was holding down rose fast and spilled out of her, onto her fastidious, angry self.

"Girlfriend—come with me now. I have some people I want you to meet. It time."

Small plain room in a tenement yard.

Tell us about yourself.
What would you like to know?
What comes to mind?
I am a Jamaican. My mother is dead. My father lives in New York. We are not in touch.
What else?
I have lived in the States, in New York, and in Europe—London and elsewhere.
You stress place, it seems.
I thought you wanted to know my history.
How do you feel . . . about what we are asking you?
What do you mean exactly?
To whom do you owe your allegiance?
I have African, English, Carib in me.
Can we trust you?
I believe things must change. . . .
Truly?
How could anyone not believe that?
There are those who do not, as you well know.
Yes, of course. I . . . if anything, I owe my allegiance to the place my grandmother made.
Place again?
It represented a labor of love—once.
Will you let us use this land?
Yes.
Are you sure?
Yes. I have thought about it. My grandmother believed in using the land to feed people. My mother as well . . . communists, I guess (smile).
We do not offer the standard form of nourishment. . . .
I am aware of that . . . but once you clear the land, you will distribute the surplus to the people around? That is what I was given to understand.
Yes; we will. But that is not our main purpose.

I know that.

Do you think you are morally superior to someone of my color?

No.

Politically?

No.

Intellectually?

No.

Are you certain?

You are the color of my grandmother.

As you well know, that could be as nothing.

I am as certain as I can be.

But?

No "but."

But it was taken in with your mother's milk . . . so to speak. To deny that is to deny reality.

I am aware of that reality.

From personal experience . . . or observation?

Both.

Do you consider yourself a fighter?

I have fought that particular reality, yes.

Could you tell me one instance of your struggle?

It's not that simple . . . that easy to tell.

Please try.

I can't at the moment . . . perhaps later.

We need to know where you stand in all this.

I have lost people . . . is that enough?

That is loss, not struggle.

The struggle comes . . . came . . . later.

How would you feel about killing someone?

What do you mean?

Under what circumstances would you kill another human being?

Why are you asking me this?

We need to know who you are. . . . Under what circumstances—

Defending myself (spoken tentatively).

What about defending your home?

Yes . . . I imagine.

What about defending a friend?

Yes (looking at Harriet).

Would you kill to eat?

You mean wring the neck of a chicken after church on Sunday? (A flash of her mother sitting on an upended box, as a chicken, headless, flailed beneath.)

No. Would you kill someone standing between you and food?

No. I don't think so.

Then you have never really been hungry.

Not for food, no. That is . . .

Yes?

Never mind.

No; please continue.

I have been without food from time to time, as few haven't . . . but I have not suffered the lifelong consequences of hunger, as many have. . . . My bones are not bent.

Would you kill if your child got polio, and you knew this was a result of government policy, and you knew exactly whom to blame?

I don't have any children.

Imagine that you did.

Yes. I'll try. (Thoughts of missed motherhood flooded her; facts, myths she had heard. Weren't women supposed to accomplish superhuman feats when their children were endangered? Would she? Had her own mother? She had read about a female alligator who returned to her nest and found it fenced around with anchor steel. The humans nearby wanted to see if her eggs would hatch and the babies develop without nurture. They got more than they expected as the mother alligator shredded the fence with teeth and tail . . . roaring. Would she have done such a thing? She had heard of the cobra who slithered into a village in Turkey to find her nest empty—not knowing the villagers sensed a flash flood and moved the eggs to a higher ground. She spat into the barrel which held the village water supply, then slithered away only to find her eggs by chance, recognizing them instantly. Back to the village she stretched her body to its tautest and embraced the water barrel, collapsing its sides. Would she have such a keen sense of justice and the strength to carry it out? Had she known the blood clots were the beginning of a child with half a brain would she be angry?) Yes. I think I would. I am trying to be honest. You are asking things which are difficult to answer. It is easy to feel I do not own any of this.

Can you believe we love the children of this island?

Yes.

You have recently returned to your homeland.

I have been back the past two years or so.

And what have you done with your time?

I thought Harriet told you.

Tell us in your own words.

I have been teaching . . . reading and writing and history. I have been teaching children in a secondary school downtown . . . near to where Harriet and I live. I have approximately forty students.

Do you enjoy teaching?

I care about my students, yes. I . . .

So . . . it's not just place with you, then?

That was your assumption.

Sorry . . . please go on.

My students range in age from thirteen to sixteen. Some of them have responsibilities I do not have . . . I am thirty-five. Responsibilities to other children, for one thing. But you know this sort of thing. Some of their mouths have no front teeth. I have all my teeth, save one.

Do they trust you?

Some do. Some don't. Why should they?

What drew you to this work . . . back to this place?

Nothing pure and simple. . . . My own needs, for the most part.

Say more, please.

I returned to this island to mend . . . to bury . . . my mother. . . . I returned to this island because there was nowhere else. . . . I could live no longer in borrowed countries, on borrowed time. There is danger here—in sounding . . . seeming foolish.

That concerns you.

Seems to.

What drew you to this work . . . teaching?

I am suited for little else.

Like what?

I don't know . . . nursing, for example. The laying on of hands.

What history do you bring to your students?

The history of their . . . our homeland.

How have you found this history?

I have educated myself since my return. Spoken with the old people . . . leafed through the archives downtown . . . spent time at the university library . . . one thing leads to another. I have studied the conch knife excavated at the Arawak site in White Marl . . . the shards of hand-thrown pots . . . the petroglyphs hidden in the bush . . . listened to the stories about Nanny and taken them to heart. I have seen the flock of white birds fly out at sunset from Nannytown . . . duppies, the old people say.

Duppies?

Ghosts; the spirits of Maroons.

What else . . . what other sources?

Stories of Anansi . . . Oshun . . . Shàngó . . . I have walked the cane . . . poked through the ruins . . . rusted machines marked Glasgow . . . standing as they were left. I have swum underwater off the cays.

History can be found underwater.

Yes—some history is only underwater.

This is a departure for you.

Yes.

It says here (glancing at a folder on the table) that you did graduate work in England . . . the Renaissance . . . am I correct?

Yes. It feels like a very long time ago.

Don't apologize. I did a tripos in classics at Girton, so

I am hardly in a position to judge. Tell me, why did you do it?

Because it did not concern me . . . I was looking for something to take me out of myself . . . it worked, for a while.

No stake?

Oh, I suppose . . . a stake in showing them, proving I could do it.

Yes. I left my mother's village empty-handed, and returned weighted down with paper—to be framed and nailed above her bed, next to her cross and a goldminer's photograph, my father. . . . Anyway, did you?

What?

Prove it? To them; yourself?

Something pulled me away . . . I didn't finish . . . but, yes, I suppose I proved it. Tell me something?

What?

Does your mother know about your affiliation?

My mother died at the funeral of a friend . . . several years ago.

I'm sorry.

Indeed . . . now, you tell me something?

Yes?

This new sort of history . . . that you have taken on; is there proof involved in it as well?

It's not as simple as that. I am in it. It involves me . . . the practice of rubbing lime and salt in the backs of whipped slaves . . . the ambush tactics of Cudjoe . . . the promised flight of Alexander Bedward in rapture back to Africa . . . cruelty . . . resistance . . . grace. I'm not outside this history—it's a matter of recognition . . . memory . . . emotion. When I study Tom Cringle's silk cotton tree, I wonder about the fact that I have never been able to bear a necklace around my throat . . . not even a scarf.

How would you sum up this experience of teaching, learning?

It's the best thing I have done. It's the only thing I have

done. That would be one way of saying it—but too tidy.

Say more, please.

I have told you the best I can. I am not a missionary, nor a Peace Corps volunteer. I have not been sent from somewhere. I came here because I could not go elsewhere. Perhaps you would judge all this too much an individual statement . . . a confession of need . . . personal . . . mawkish . . . I don't know.

Do you love these children?

Yes.

Would you kill for them?

Are we back to that?

Never mind. . . . If you have been here for the past two years, then you realize all progress is backward, and the gaps become wider. People are being left for dead—more than ever. You have no doubt observed these things? The increased madness, fury, in the streets?

Yes.

You know then that the rivers run red . . . and the underground aquifers are colored . . . from the waste of the bauxite mines and the aluminum refineries? We do not speak of past here, but present, future.

These things are connected.

Of course, but this is now . . . immediate. Children drink from this water every day of their lives. Women wash in it. Men fish from it. Brew coffee. Clean tripe. Immerse believers. The waste leaches into the land. And people for miles around are covered with a fine dust which invades them. Do you have any idea of the power of such things . . . for future generations . . . for the future of your homeland? Do you not realize that this is but one example of contamination from the outside? And you are but one infected nation? Do you realize the contempt in which you are held? And that your leaders invite it? What good is your history to a child with bone cancer . . . polio . . . TB . . . a damaged brain?

My history brought me to this room. The history I have

learned . . . rather, recognized . . . since my return is something else. I know only that the loss, the forgetting . . . of resistance . . . of tenderness . . . is a terrible thing. Look, I want to restore something to these children. . . . And of course you are right: what good is imagination . . . whatever the imagery available to it . . . to a dying child? A child damaged beyond imagining? I . . . it seems I contradict myself.

Not really . . . what you feel is true.

Yes.

We—neither of us—want for these children a harsh, unnatural end.

No . . . I told you, you can use the land. I have given this a lot of thought.

You realize you could be held accountable . . . even if you claim not to be one of us.

Yes; I do.

You are certain, then?

My mother told me to help my people. At the moment this is the closest I can come.

Perhaps you will go further . . . sometimes it is the only way. We are not thugs, you know. . . . You speak of the knowledge of resistance . . . the loss of this knowledge. I ask you to think of Bishop. Rodney. Fanon. Lumumba. Malcolm. First. Luthuli. Garvey. Mxembe. Marley. Moloise. Think of these who are gone—and ask yourself how, why . . . ? Now, I must return to my own country. I will be back. *Amandla*.

The two women shook hands.

11

FILM NOIR

In their faint photographs
mottled with chemicals,
like the left hand of some spinster aunt,
they have drifted to the edge
of verandas in Whistlerian
white, their jungle turned tea-brown—
even its spiked palms—
their features pale,
to be pencilled in:
bone-collared gentlemen
with spiked mustaches
and their wives embayed in the wickerwork
armchairs, all looking colored
from the distance of a century
beginning to groan sideways from the ax stroke!

The bay horses blacken
like spaniels, the front lawn a beige
carpet, brown moonlight and a moon
so sallow, so pharmaceutical
that her face is a feverish child's,
some malarial angel
whose grave still cowers
under a fury of bush,
a mania of wild yams
wrangling to hide her from ancestral churchyards.

                    —DEREK WALCOTT, "Jean Rhys"

Clare slithered beneath her grandmother's house, drawing her head through widows' webs, pulling herself through the hard black leavings of rats, hands scraping against fragments of shells embedded in the ground, which signaled the explosive birth of the island. The sound of a scorpion readying its sting stopped her. She took a book, the closest thing to hand, and flattened her enemy. The ooze of the scorpion stained the already rat-bitten book, bits clinging where the cloth puckered from damp.

Under this house she found solace from the rest of the company. She found her mother's things from childhood—schoolbooks, thread-spool dollies, vehicles with wheels of shoe-polish tins. Her mother's schoolbooks—history, literature, geography—opened their wormed pages to a former world. Things, beings, existed in their rightful place—destiny, order were honored. God's impatient hand feared. Clare wiped the remains of the scorpion from the book and gathered her mother's girlhood into a crocus sack. Working a broad piece of shell free of the earth, she began to scrape the packed ground.

"Girlfriend?" Harriet's voice traveled into the underground.

"I'm here," Clare called back.

"We need you out here now."

"Cyaan wait a few minutes?"

"No. There is a new plan. We will have to leave soon."

"I'll be there."

Clare tucked the ends of the crocus sack into the loosened earth, placing the piece of shell on top.

Jamaica, which is about an hour and a half south of Miami by jet, is a little smaller than Connecticut and has some of the most varied terrain in the world. It not only has all the beaches, sparkling clear water and foliage you would expect to find on a tropical island, but it also has mountains that rise to more than 7,000 feet, waterfalls, caves, wide open areas that resemble the African plain and even arid sections that will pass for desert.

In addition, it has an abundance of Spanish and British colonial buildings dating back to the 1500s. It has concrete and glass cities, elegant suburban homes, ramshackle slums and villages with thatched huts. It also has a racially mixed population of many hues and ethnic distinctions, which . . . includes a number of people willing to serve as extras. The national language is English, and you can drink the water.

—Special to *The New York Times,* August 27, 1984

Two whitemen sat in a rumshop, out of place, drinking too-pink daiquiris. The bartender, used to men ordering their rum straight, white, in water tumblers, was hard-pressed to make the likeness of a tourist drink and was heavy-handed with the grenadine, which he snatched from his wife's snowball cart, parked in the yard behind the shop. The cart bore the legend SO JAH SEH and was waiting repair for a broken wheel.

"Christ . . . they call this a daiquiri? I thought they invented the bloody things."

"No . . . no, that was Cuba . . . before the revolution."

"Ever work there?"

"Yeah, babe. In 'fifty-eight. War movie. What a place . . . shit, you could get anything. Anything your little heart desired. . . ."

The two men sat at the only table in the rumshop, under a calendar sporting a naked woman and advertising assurance.

"Still, you'd think they'd have learned to make a decent one by now. . . . I wonder if I can get anything to eat?"

"I wouldn't."

Both men were suntanned and sunglassed. There was an impatience about them.

"Christ," said the first one again. "Christ . . . if they can't make a bloody daiquiri, how in hell are they going to provide us with what we need?"

"You think this place is bad . . . Jesus! Have I seen places . . . the Congo—"

"We're not going to hear about the African bloody Queen again."

"Sorry." The American pronounced the word with British intonation.

"And all the bloody dysentery and the bloody bugs and running out of bloody gin—or was that the film?"

"Okay . . . you made your point. As far as this place is concerned, don't worry. They'll manage. You can't beat the prices. And, besides, they need the money . . . real bad. They'll shape up . . . they have to. They're trapped. All tied up by the IMF. All thanks to Manley and his bleeding heart."

"We are the international expert, aren't we."

"I just love the way you English ask questions which are statements."

"Sorry."

"And how you say sorry on any conceivable occasion."

"Sorry . . . we *are* bloody testy today. Is it the heat? Or this bloody drink that tastes like cough mixture?"

"Fuck. Can't you talk about anything besides your goddam drink? It's nothing. I'm probably getting too old for the work is all . . . too much running around. Anyway, this gig shouldn't be too bad. As the saying goes, they need us a helluva lot more than we need them, babe. They'll even give us their fucking army if we need it—God help us—talk about the gang that couldn't shoot straight. They'll give it to us for a price. But not a bad price . . . not at all."

"With helicopters marked MADE IN USA?"

"Who cares? Just be grateful this isn't Haiti."

"Ah, yes, *The Comedians* . . . Richard Burton . . . Elizabeth Taylor . . . and you chasing zombies off the set."

"Fuck you. Just be glad you're working with someone who's got experience in this part of the world."

"About the army . . . there isn't any danger, is there? I mean, they *are* offering the army to us strictly as . . ."

"Ah, a real question. Now you want my expertise, huh? Just like the rest of the babies in this business. Afraid your butt might end up in a sling. . . . No. I don't think so, if you're asking what I think you're asking. No.

"Jamaicans will do anything for a buck. . . . Look around you . . . the hotels . . . the private resorts where you have to get an invite . . . the reggae festivals for white kids . . . Jesus! The cancer spas for rich people. Everyone from the hookers to the prime minister, babe. These people are used to selling themselves. I don't think they know from revolution. That brief shit with Manley was the exception. Oh, the poor followed him; the poor occasionally protest about prices, shortages, that kind of thing—"

"Where?"

"*New York Times,* business section, mostly."

"Oh."

"Yeah, but not any real threat . . . none at all. And even the poor. . . . Jesus Christ! Where could you find people demonstrating, burning tires, blocking roads, and then accepting tips from tourists to let them pass?"

"Just about anywhere, I expect."

"Nah. I don't think so. Anyway, babe, about your fear, about revolution . . . the class system wouldn't permit. I mean, they're more English than the English in that regard. At least, the ones on top are. The ones who call the shots."

"Do you have any personal—"

"I worked here on *Dr. No*—didn't I tell you? Later, on a couple of TV shoots. . . . I had a buddy on *The Harder They Come*. I know what I'm talking about.

"But if there's trouble, we're well set. We have enough natives employed as scouts and advisers, so-called, that if there was a problem we'd be the first to know.

"These people may not know much, but they know how to protect him that's got the bucks.

"*Burn!* Now there was a movie."

His companion let him have his reminiscence. Brando. Martinique. Revolution. Sixties enthusiasm for turning everything upside down. Christ! This was the eighties.

"Still, it's a fucking marvelous place, isn't it." The Englishman broke the silence. "I found a location looks just like the fucking South of France, except for all the black bums on the beach."

"They'll stay away for a per diem."

"Right. We have an island. Landscape. Extras up the ass. Weather. And a fucking army complete with helicopters—"

"Say, where is that guy, anyway?"

"Why don't you check with the bartender; and while you're at it, get us a couple more of these—but tell him to go easy on the grenadine."

The American got up and walked over to the bar, a distance of about five feet—and that was stretching it. The bartender was rubbing a piece of rag across the zinc surface. "Sah?" the man acknowledged, not indicating by his tone, or manner, that he had heard any of the conversation.

"Give us a couple more of these, will you? And go easy on the grenadine."

The man poured white rum almost to the brim of each tumbler and slid in one ice cube each.

"Say, do you have a number where we can reach this guy?"

"Sah?" The bartender rubbed slowly across the zinc, carefully avoiding the two beading tumblers. Ice melting fast.

"The guy you scouted for us . . . the one we paid you fifty dollars for?"

"Oh, De Watchman . . . no, sah, De Watchman him don't have no numba, sah. But him will be in soon now . . . soon come, yes, sah."

"Well, we don't have all day."

"Yes, sah. Me understand, sah. But him will be ya, sah."

"How can you be so certain?"

"Oh, him come in ya so same time every day, sah. Him sweep, me give him to drink."

The American took charge. "Okay. But you better be right. If he's not here by the time we finish these, then we'll find us another boy, understand?"

"Indeed, sah."

"How much do we owe you?"

"Ah . . . four drink, sah? That will be twenty dollar, sah—American, not Jamaican. For a hundred more, me will throw in mi mumma and cure fe you cancer as well."

"You talk about finding a place like the South of France," the American said back at the table, assuming his companion had heard everything spoken at the bar. "Well," he continued, "that won't exactly fit with this shoot."

"Whose idea was it anyway?"

"You mean the whole thing?"

"To do a picture about them."

"Good story. Goodwill. You know."

"Some producer—"

"Some producer down here at someone's hideaway found

a book to read himself to sleep and thought it would be a good idea. It's actually pretty solid. Lots of action."

"Right." He was unconvinced.

The doors to the rumshop, slatted and scalloped like the doors to a western saloon, swung open. Preceded by his iron walking staff, De Watchman entered, draped in his split crocus sack, snake-haired, walking up to the bar.

"Beg pardon, sah"—the bartender interrupted the two white men—"Here is de man me did tell you about."

At the bartender's signal, the two walked up to the bar to meet De Watchman.

"Okay." The American spoke. "You look pretty good to me. Can you howl for us?"

"Sah?"

"Howl, you know."

The man's stench began to fill the tiny establishment, and the two white men edged back as far as they could.

"Sah, if me should howl, den every dog in Kingston gwan come." He smiled at the men, toothless.

"Okay." The American relented. "But would you be willing to howl for the part? That is, if we put you in a movie, would you howl for us?"

"Sah?"

"A movie. You know. You have seen a movie, haven't you?"

"I don't know, sah."

"Jesus Christ!"

"No need fe call him name, sah."

"No; okay. I think you'll be fine. Your hair, the look in your eyes. Look, Brian. Look, Watchman, I don't want you to change a thing. We'll pick you up here in one week—understand? Same time. There's a hundred dollars for you if you come with us."

"What you want me fe do, sah?"

"Just sit in a tree and howl. That's all. You can do that, can't you?"

"Yes, sah."

*

205

The truck had reached its destination. The group got off, quickly, gathered their weapons, and set off into bush. It was night. Dark and cool. The air thin. Harriet grasped Clare's hand. Walk safe, girlfriend, walk safe. Clare squeezed her friend's hand in return and moved off on her own.

As they lay in preparation for their act, hidden by dark and green, separate, silent—as silent as Maroons—they watched the scene below them. The valley was lit by a harsh, unnatural light, sending deep shadows into the hollows of landscape, creating false contrasts. They lay in night, beneath them was day. On a flat, cleared space in this light people mingled in old-fashioned dress. Hovering above these anachronistic people men sat on cranes, shouting directions, advising them, the ones below, the actors, on movement, carriage, how things had been in Jamaica several hundred years before. They were a lively, busy crowd.

"Let's go, people! Let's make it real!" The people stopped moving. "Action!"

Two figures stood out in the costumed group. One, a woman, the actress called in whenever someone was needed to play a Black heroine, any Black heroine, whether Sojourner Truth or Bessie Smith, this woman wore a pair of leather breeches and a silk shirt—designer's notion of the clothes that Nanny wore. Dear Nanny, the Coromantee warrior, leader of the Windward Maroons, whom one book described as an old woman naked except for a necklace made from the teeth of whitemen—sent by the orishas to deliver her people. Wild Nanny, sporting furies through the Blue Mountains. Old. Dark. Small. But such detail was out of the question, given these people even knew the truth. Or cared. Facing the elegant actress was a strapping man, former heavyweight or running back, dressed as Cudjoe, tiny humpbacked soul.

These two spoke back and forth, exchanging phrases of love in the screenwriter's version of Coromantee—which was, for all intents and purposes, pidgin. The dialogue coach a retired civil servant.

Clare was lying flat in a bitterbush.

To the side of the scene, beyond the principals, beneath the gaze of the technical people, in the fiercely lit night, stood De Watchman. Got up as Sasabonsam. Forest God. His human body covered in a suit of long red hair, fiery, thick. Lord Jesus he was hot. Sweat making the costume stick to his naked skin.

"In the tree, man, up in the tree!" The director shouted through his bullhorn from the crane. "We're going to shoot the scene where the monster attacks Nanny, and Cudjoe rescues her."

De Watchman hauled his heavy hot self into the breadfruit tree and dangled his legs, waiting further direction. The bright-green fruit swung around him, some dropping as the tree settled with his weight.

"Howl!"

"Sah?"

"Howl! Howl! I want you to bellow as loud as you can. Try to wake the dead. . . . Remember, you're not human. Action!"

De Watchman complied, as they had rehearsed him, and the air of the valley was split with his huge wails. Clare imagined she could feel them through her belly, resting on the earth. His eyes, fitted with lenses, reflecting red, a nocturnal glare, as the light suddenly dimmed. He became the focus, his bellows carrying into the darkening country.

Then the light was gone. And the people hidden in the bush, waiting for the soft signal of the abeng, were confused. This was not meant to happen; it had not been in the plan.

Sasabonsam did not let up in the pitch dark. Had his noise extinguished light? His howls became larger, longer— for a time his noise masked other noises. Of the actors and technicians, retreating the scene and locking themselves in trailers, as they had been warned. Someone opened a bottle of rum and passed it hand to hand, as they sat on the floor of an Airstream, waiting for this to pass.

Those hidden in the bush could do little but listen to the chaos of the forest god, until a new sound drowned him out. And lights came over them from above. Who had been the quashee? some asked. Lights played and skidded across their hiding places, as helicopters spun into the valley. Lights sliding over, guns hot. Spraying the breadfruit tree. Sasabonsam fell, silent. Spraying across the bushes.

Some returned the fire—but were no match for the invaders. Some could not—surprise and sadness held them still. There was no time left to them.

Shots found the bitterbush.

O je t'adore, O je t'adore, O je t'adore
Poor-me-one, poor-me-one, poor-me-one
Tres-tontos-son, tres-tontos-son, tres-tontos-son
Kitty-woo, kitty-woo, kitty-woo
Whip-whip-whip-whip-whip-whip-whip-whip-whip-whip
Back-raw, back-raw, back-raw, back-raw, back-raw

She remembered language.
Then   it was gone.

cutacoo, cutacoo, cutacoo
coo, cu, cu, coo
coo, cu, cu, coo
piju, piju, piju
cuk, cuk, cuk, cuk
tuc-tuc-tuc-tuc-tuc
eee-kah, eee-kah, eee-kah
krrr
krrr
krrr-re-ek
cawak, cawak, cawak
hoo hoo hoo hoo hoo hoo hoo hoo hoo hoo hoo
be be be be be be be be be be be be be be be
kut ktu ktu kut ktu ktu
cwa cwa cwa   cwaah cwaah cwaah

Day broke.

GLOSSARY

afu: yellow yam; Ashanti
bacalao: dried salted codfish
backra: white; white-identified. Probably from the West African *mbakara,* he who surrounds or governs. Some Jamaicans believe the word derives from back-raw, the condition of a slave's back after whipping.
bammy: flat cassava cake
battyman: male homosexual; pejorative
black-up: drunk
blood-clat: very strong swear word; from the blood cloth used to wipe a slave's back after whipping
bluefoot: stranger
bredda: brother
brukins: party
bullah cake: flat, tough molasses cake
bunga: African
busha: overseer

bwai: boy

cho-cho: chayote; also called mirliton

Chrismus fat: rain at Christmastime

coo ya: look here

cotta: round cushion of cloth, used to balance burdens on the head

craven: greedy

cropover: holiday to celebrate the harvest of sugar cane

cuffy: upstart

cya: care

cyaan: can't

cyar: car

dry-jump: to be moved in a religious service but not to possess a true spirit

duppy: ghost, spirit

eidon: the spirit or spirits of unbaptized babies

Ethiopian apple: common name for otaheite apple, brought to Jamaica by Captain Bligh

facey: impertinent

fiah: fire

foy-eyed: possessing second sight

fufu: yellow yam; Ashanti

higgler: peddler

itation: a meditation on Jah; Rastafarian term

jackass rope: cheap, rough tobacco

Jamaican tall: a variety of palm tree

Jonkonnu: name given merrymakers, who dress up and dance in the streets at Christmastime; possibly from *gens inconnu*

jook: stick, poke (v.t.)

labrish: gossip

licklemos': almost

mauger: skinny; scrawny

mek: make; let, allow

nyam: to eat; the Ashanti word means move quickly

pickney: child; children

patoo: owl

quashee: betrayer; from the slave Quashee

rhyging: thoroughly bad, worthless; from the bandit of the same name

rolling calf: in Jamaican belief, a creature who is motivated by an unquiet spirit (duppy). This creature marauds by night and may take the form of a calf, dog, hog, or cat, as well as other animals. The creature drags a chain from its neck. The *rolling* in its name means roaming, wandering. One rids oneself of the rolling calf by flogging it with one's left hand.

say: know

shipmate: shipmates were slaves who made the crossing from Africa on the same slave ship. The relationship of shipmate to shipmate formed a strong bond, a kinship, particularly since, under slavery, the destruction of clan and family was profound.

sinting: something

smaddy: somebody

spliff: ganja joint

talawa: powerful

teenager roach: small cockroach

watchman: the piece of salt pork atop a pot of rice and peas

wunna: you, your

ya: here; hear

yard: close grouping of houses, found both in country and city, modeled on the grouping of slave huts, which were in turn modeled on the grouping of family dwellings in West African cultures

yeye: eye(s)

ABOUT THE AUTHOR

Michelle Cliff, who grew up in Jamaica and the United States, was educated in New York and at the University of London. She has received exceptional critical praise for her previous books, *Claiming an Identity They Taught Me to Despise, Abeng,* and *The Land of Look Behind,* which was chosen to represent the United States at the Frankfurt Book Fair. The National Endowment for the Arts as well as the Artists Foundation of Massachusetts have granted her fellowships in creative writing and fiction, respectively. Internationally known through her essays, articles, lectures, and workshops on issues of racism and feminism, Michelle Cliff lives in Santa Cruz, California.